PRAISE FOR THE

Dragon Slippers

SERIES

"Clever, well-plotted and good fun."
—*Kirkus Reviews* on *Dragon Slippers*

"A magical, fun-filled page-turner. . . . A far cry from an
old-school Cinderella story." —*Bookpage* on *Dragon Slippers*

"The exciting fairy-tale action and vivid scenes . . . are captivating."
—*Booklist* on *Dragon Slippers*

"Reminiscent of works by Patricia C. Wrede or Gail Carson Levine . . .
fast paced and entertaining, and filled with honorable, evil, and quirky
characters—both human and dragon." —*SLJ* on *Dragon Flight*

"George creates a very satisfying sequel that adds just the right touches
to complete the story. Creel is still a dynamic protagonist whose
spunk and intellect ring true." —*VOYA* on *Dragon Flight*

"A tasty snack for dragon lovers."
—*Kirkus Reviews* on *Dragon Spear*

Books by Jessica Day George

Dragon Slippers
Dragon Flight
Dragon Spear

Sun and Moon, Ice and Snow
Princess of the Midnight Ball
Princess of Glass

DRAGON SPEAR

Jessica Day George

7.99

9/12

BLOOMSBURY

NEW YORK BERLIN LONDON

Fic
Geo

First published in the United States of America in May 2009
by Bloomsbury Books for Young Readers
Paperback edition published in September 2010
www.bloomsburykids.com

For information about permission to reproduce selections from this book, write to
Permissions, Bloomsbury BFYR, 175 Fifth Avenue, New York, New York 10010

The Library of Congress has cataloged the hardcover edition as follows:
George, Jessica Day.
Dragon spear / by Jessica Day George. — 1st U.S. ed.
     p.   cm.
Sequel to: Dragon flight.
Summary: Creel's adventures continue when she, her brother, and her betrothed travel across
the seas to visit their dragon friends and become involved in a battle against an alien group of dragons
that has kidnapped Queen Velika, endangering her and her expected litter of hatchlings.
ISBN-13: 978-1-59990-369-9 • ISBN-10: 1-59990-369-5 (hardcover)
[1. Dragons—Fiction. 2. Kings, queens, rulers, etc.—Fiction. 3. Fantasy.] I. Title.
PZ7.G293317Ds 2009   [Fic]—dc22   2008044414

ISBN 978-1-59990-516-7 (paperback)

Book design by Donna Mark
Typeset by Westchester Book Composition
Printed in the U.S.A. by Worldcolor Fairfield, Pennsylvania
3 5 7 9 10 8 6 4 2

All papers used by Bloomsbury Publishing, Inc., are natural, recyclable products
made from wood grown in well-managed forests. The manufacturing processes
conform to the environmental regulations of the country of origin.

For Amy Finnegan:
friend and writer

The Islands of the North

It's a bucket of sand," I said.

"Yes, yes, it is!" Luka was still grinning at me with delight. "*Black* sand. And we got six bucketfuls!"

"How nice," I told him. I looked over at Tobin. "Did he hit his head while you were out exploring?"

The mute warrior grinned and flicked his fingers at me slowly. I had never been as adept at interpreting Tobin's hand signs as Luka or Tobin's wife, Marta, but I caught this message easily enough.

"It's a present for Shardas? Why on earth would a dragon want buckets of black sand?"

I stepped back from the incoming tide and rolled down the legs of my trousers, then picked up my bucket of crabs. We had been catching crabs to cook for supper when Luka had disappeared with Tobin, to return an hour later with the buckets of coarse, dark sand.

"Creel," Luka said, the pleased expression on his face telling me my prince was about to unspool a grand plan, "do you know how glass is made?"

"Of course," I said, somewhat stung even though I knew that he wasn't trying to make me look foolish. I was very sensitive about my poor schooling: I had grown up on a drought-stricken farm far to the north, and lately large gaps in my education had been brought to my attention by Luka's father, King Caxel. The king was not pleased that his son was marrying a commoner.

A commoner—that is to say, me.

"You, er, make glass by . . ." I trailed off, blushing. "All right: where *does* glass come from?"

Luka put the bucket down beside the others and gave my sandy hand a squeeze. His was equally dirty. "I'd be surprised if you knew; I doubt most people do," he said gently. "Glassmakers are notoriously secretive. Glass is made from sand that has been melted." Now his grin was even wider.

I blinked at him. "How hot does sand have to get before it melts?"

"Very hot. Dragonfire hot, you might say. Shardas has been talking about making his own glass, and the best way to get different colors and textures is to use different types of sand. Black sand is very rare, but it's the only way to make a true red glass."

The buckets of sand now seemed precious rather than strange. I knelt beside one and ran my fingers through the coarse grains. "How wonderful!"

The dragons had been exiled from all but a few civilized lands, forced from their caves and hoards. They had found a new home in the south, on the Far Isles, many days' flight from my home in Feravel, but the last year had not been easy for them.

They had had to excavate new caves, learn to forage for

foods, and set up their own gardens and herds of animals. A large number of the dragons had been born into slavery to the army of the desert nation of Citatie, and consequently lacked even the most basic survival skills.

Shardas, the king of the dragons, was a dear friend of mine. He loved stained glass, and had once had a magnificent hoard of stained glass windows. His mate, Velika, also loved glass, though she preferred finely blown glassware. Both of their hoards had been destroyed some time ago, and the Far Isles were not a place where they could come by either type of glass easily. Which brought us back to Luka's buckets.

I shook the sand off my fingers. "So," I said casually, trying not to reveal further ignorance, "when they say *blown glass* . . ."

"When the sand gets hot enough, it melts together until it's like taffy," Luka explained. "They make vases and goblets by blowing through a pipe with a blob of melted sand on the end, shaping it into whatever you want."

My brow furrowed. "It sounds difficult."

"I'm sure it is," he said, undaunted. "But I think that Shardas is up to the challenge."

"Of course he is," I agreed, feeling a thrill of excitement. In a few weeks we would be going to visit Shardas and Velika and the rest of the dragons on the Far Isles, and I couldn't wait.

"All right, I think I have enough crabs," I said, straightening. "We'd better get them back to Marta before she runs out of firewood."

Marta, my business partner, was waiting farther down the

beach. We were in Moralien, Tobin's birthplace, for Marta and Tobin's One Year Celebration. According to Tobin's brother Skarpin, Moralienin men were so impossible to live with that if their brides didn't kill them by the end of a year there was a month of dancing and feasting. The newlyweds give gifts to their relations as thanks for putting up with them for an entire year. Last year at their wedding Luka had proposed to me, and now at their One Year Celebration he was trying to convince me to get married in Moralien—right then—rather than being married in Feravel later in the spring.

As we cooked the crabs over the driftwood fire that Marta had prepared, Luka tried again. "My father isn't here to glare at you," he wheedled. "It'll be much more enjoyable this way."

This actually gave me pause. Not being glared at by my future father-in-law during my wedding was tempting.

"I don't have my dress with me," I said, firming my resolve. I was a dressmaker, and for a dressmaker to get married in anything less than splendor was probably both a sin and against the law.

He appealed to Marta. "Talk to her, Marta. We've waited a year already, and now we're going to be in the Far Isles for months."

"Oh, no!" I rounded on her, shaking my finger. "I helped you sew *two* wedding gowns, don't you dare try to convince me that one of my traveling gowns will be fine."

Marta sighed. "She has a point." She sat down on a log bench beside Tobin and pulled a fur rug up over her legs. "And Shardas would be crushed if he wasn't there to stand for her family."

"Aha! See!" I poked Luka's nose. "You can wait until the spring." Secretly, I wasn't too keen on the long betrothal either, but if I was going to be married in front of every titled wealthy in Feravel, plus ambassadors from Roulain, Citatie, Moralien, and who knew where else, not to mention the glaring King Caxel, I wanted to make certain that everything was perfect. Getting my dragon friends there was another complication that I still hadn't worked out, and I wished that Marta hadn't said anything about Shardas being there. King Caxel had banned all dragons from Feravel, no exceptions, and I would rather have Shardas at my side than most of my blood relatives.

"I might be dead by then." Luka groaned. He pulled a fur rug over us both as we waited for the crabs to be ready. Even with a roaring fire, Moralien in early autumn was cold.

"You'll be fine," I told him, leaning against his shoulder and tucking my side of the rug around my legs.

"How do you know?" He made his voice sound faint and long-suffering. "It's months away. Anything could happen. Anything!"

The Invasion of the Palace

There really was no way around it: my aunt was dumber than two turnips in a rain barrel.

I'd told Luka and Marta this when I related the story of how three years ago she had decided to leave me for the Carlieff dragon to eat. Which is how I ended up walking to the King's Seat to get work as a dressmaker, befriending several dragons, and wearing a pair of dragonskin slippers that started a war.

But I don't think either of them really believed me.

That is, they didn't believe me until we returned to the King's Seat, fattened on Moralienin crab and spiced honey bread, to find my aunt ensconced in the New Palace, with my uncle and all of my cousins in tow, of course.

Luka was just helping me off my horse when the double doors to the palace swung open and my brother, Hagen, came hurrying out, followed by two of my cousins. I shouted with delight and ran to embrace my little brother, who was now more than a head taller than I.

Hugging my cousins next, whom I now had only benevolent feelings toward since we no longer shared a bed, I exclaimed over how well they looked. Then it hit me that if my cousins had come all the way to the King's Seat, my aunt couldn't be far behind.

"Oh, no!" I let go of my cousin Leesel with dismay. "Hagen, please tell me—"

"Dear, *dear* Creelisel!"

My stomach dropped to my shoes as my dear, *dear* aunt Reena appeared at the top of the broad steps. She was wearing a long, purple gown that even from this distance I could tell was the work of Mistress Lelane, my mother's former dressmaking rival in Carlieff Town. Aunt Reena came fluttering down the steps, her arms spread wide, but stopped with a little shriek just a few paces away.

"*What are you wearing?*" Her ruddy cheeks went even redder and she yanked the shawl off my cousin Pella's shoulders and tried to wrap it around my waist. Then she looked anxiously around the courtyard to see who else might have seen me wearing trousers.

"Aunt Reena, *Aunt Reena!*" I fended her off as best I could. "My trousers are fine; I've been riding, after all." I straightened my tunic. I had enjoyed wearing trousers in Citatie the year before, and continued to wear them when I went riding, although I'd gotten some shocked looks at first. Marta and our apprentice, Alle, had started wearing them as well, though, and the trend was beginning to spread.

"Well, I can see it's a good thing I've come." She began to drag me toward the palace. "Not just because of your appalling costume, but the steward is being very curt with us. You will need to speak to him firmly. As the only family of a princess, we deserve much finer rooms. Don't worry: I will coach you in what to say. You will be his mistress someday, and he must learn to respect you. Now, about our chambers—"

I dug my heels into the stones of the courtyard. "I am not a princess, and I will not be mistress of the palace one day," I told her as calmly as I could, shaking off her arm. "I am a dressmaker, and I am marrying the king's *second* son. Crown Princess Isla is your official hostess, and *how did you know I was marrying a prince anyway?*"

This last, desperate question was aimed more at my brother, Hagen, the only member of my family I had told of my impending wedding. My parents had died four years ago, and knowing my aunt's aspirations to wealth all too well, I had instructed Hagen not to tell her anything until it was absolutely necessary. After the wedding, perhaps.

Hagen was standing back by Luka, looking sheepish. Luka was wide-eyed, as though he couldn't believe my aunt was real.

I knew exactly how he felt.

"I know it's not until spring, but I ordered some new clothes for the wedding already," Hagen mumbled. "And Master Raslton, the tailor, told Mistress Lelane. . . ."

Groaning, I put a hand over my eyes. Of course my aunt knew. If Mistress Lelane knew, the entire *town* knew. The only thing left was to pray that every neighbor and former schoolmate wouldn't show up at the wedding to help me celebrate.

"This is not the place to discuss your deceitfulness and lack of gratitude, Creelisel," my aunt said, reasserting her grip on my elbow. "Let me help you deal with that steward, and then you will present me to your betrothed and his father.

I hope that five months will be enough time to make all the arrangements for the wedding."

I bit back the question of what exactly I was supposed to be grateful for and ignored the comment about making arrangements, since they were, fortunately, already made. "Well, I would present you to my betrothed, Aunt Reena, but you're walking away from him."

My aunt froze in her tracks and spun around, her face turning as purple as her gown. "Oh, my goodness, I had no idea, Your Highness . . ." She trailed off, faced with a real dilemma. Standing beside Luka, who needed a haircut and was dressed in old riding leathers, was Tobin with his shaved and tattooed head. There were also a couple of grooms nearby whose livery was cleaner than Luka's. Which one was the prince?

I didn't let my aunt suffer long, not wanting to be cruel despite my horror at seeing her here. I took her arm, more gently than she had taken mine, and led her over to Luka. He bowed and kissed her hand and declared himself thrilled to meet my dear aunt at last, covering his astonishment with years of diplomacy lessons. Then I introduced him to my brother and cousins, and Marta and Tobin came forward to greet everyone.

In addition to Pella and Leesel, there were six younger cousins and my long-suffering uncle, who appeared next on the steps of the palace. There was a great deal of hugging, and remarks on how tall everyone had gotten, and then I introduced Luka and my friends again. My uncle pulled me aside during the flutter to whisper in my ear.

"Sorry, Creel, but once she heard the news there was no stopping her."

"It's all right," I said, giving his arm a squeeze. "Really, it's my fault: I should have sent you proper invitations to the wedding." I wrinkled my nose. "I, er, just wasn't prepared for you all to arrive so . . . early."

He hesitated. "No, it's not that. . . . I'm sure I'll be able to talk her out of it by the wedding."

My feeling of alarm reached a crescendo. "Talk her out of what?"

The youngest of my cousins, who had been a babe in arms when last I saw her, raced over and grabbed the ends of my sash. "We gonna live in palace, we gonna live in palace," she sang. "And mawwy pwinces!"

"That," my uncle said with a grimace, "Reena is determined to, er . . ."

He was unable to finish his sentence, but I didn't need him to. My aunt's ultimate dream when she had left me at the dragon's cave had been for the Lord of Carlieff's son to rescue me and carry me off to live in their manor—along with my doting family.

I thought I might faint.

Equally dumbstruck, Luka took my arm and led the parade into the palace. As we walked through the doors I whispered to him my aunt's plan to take up permanent residence, and he gave a small nod.

"Judging from what you've said about her, I suspected as much," he said. "But don't worry, we can work it out."

"How?"

The answer would have to wait, though, because the steward was waiting for us. Then a footman came forward to tell us that King Caxel was waiting for Luka in the council chamber, and a maid asked if I would like to have a bath and rest before returning to my shop. Aunt Reena was pushing me from behind, hissing at me to take all the servants "in hand."

Much to my embarrassment, I simply froze in place. I had only come to the palace in the first place because I had a gift for Princess Isla from the wife of Tobin's clan chief. But now the thought of introducing my family to my disapproving future father-in-law pushed the gift to the back of my mind. I just wanted to run straight to my shop and hide.

I was saved by Isla herself, who came floating down the grand staircase at the far end of the hall in a pale blue gown trimmed with lace—one of my creations, of course. Her smile never faltered as she kissed Luka and me, hugged Marta and Tobin, and welcomed my aunt and uncle and their children as though it were a great honor.

"I'm so sorry that I wasn't here to greet you when you arrived," she said. "But now please let me help you get settled. I understand that the steward has assigned you rooms and it looks like you have changed out of your traveling things. . . . Are the rooms to your liking?" She cocked her head to one side and looked at my aunt.

My jaw dropped as Aunt Reena—the woman who had no qualms about brazenly moving herself into the royal palace—blushed, h'mmmed, and was at a loss for words! My uncle put his arm around his wife, smiled at Isla, and told her that their rooms were perfect, thank you.

"In fact," he continued easily, as his wife continued to gape and stutter in the face of a real royal, "we're still quite tired. I think we'll go have a nice, long rest. Keep the children out from underfoot."

Isla smiled back. "Lovely. The dinner gong will sound in three hours' time, and we can all get to know one another over dinner. Creel, you can use that little room next to my dressing room to bathe and change, because of course you'll want to stay for dinner." She waved cheerfully to the young ones as my uncle led the entire brood away.

I collapsed against Luka with a small moan.

"Steady," he said, putting his arm at my waist to hold me up.

"Creel," Marta said in a faint voice, "I shall never again accuse you of exaggeration."

Tobin signed something to me, and I managed to smile. "You have no idea," I told him.

Before First Light

"So a dragon will really come to meet the boat?" Hagen gave my packs a wistful look. "And you'll fly all the way to the Far Isles?"

"That's right," I said, distracted. I had an odd number of stockings in front of me, and could not figure out where the mate for the blue one I was holding had gone. "It's still a long flight, days actually, but it would take months by ship." I crawled under my bed and located the other stocking.

Hagen had been sleeping on the sofa in the workroom behind the shop for the past two weeks. He had no desire to watch our aunt swanning around the palace, her confidence restored after King Caxel's surprisingly gracious welcome. I had asked my cousins if they wanted to stay in the shop as well, but unfortunately they had inherited my aunt's aspirations and were eager to sleep in a palace.

It had been a rough two weeks since our return from Moralien.

I had had to convince my aunt (more than once) that I would not be a princess until I married Luka, and having the servants address me as such was inappropriate, inaccurate, and possibly illegal. Miles had kindly stepped in for me and explained that my becoming a princess through marriage did not bestow any titles or estates on my aunt or her children. He had had to prove his argument by using the law books, royal pedigree charts, and, I believe, several maps, and emerged from the palace library on Aunt Reena's heels looking stunned.

I had invited Pella and Leesel to stand with Marta and Alle as my attendants, and measured them for their gowns. I put my foot down, however, over changing the design of the gowns to one created by my aunt, featuring far too much lace, gold bullion embroidery, and feathers for my taste. I had also put my foot down over adding crowns or gold underskirts to my cousins' ensembles to help them attract noble suitors.

Pella and Leesel had asked about working in my shop, and I had brought them in for a few days to learn how things were done. But on the third day, Alle went out to buy fabrics and Marta and I went to personally deliver the Duchess of Mordrel's new gown, as she was our oldest patroness and a good friend. When we returned we found that Aunt Reena had arrived, attempted to fire Alle for taking too long at the warehouse, and was in the process of approving or throwing away the gown designs in my notebook. Meanwhile, Pella and Leesel ignored the customers so that they could try on the finished gowns themselves. My younger cousins had unspooled all the ribbons in the back room and were making a giant net with them, to "catch a horrible, ugly dragon." We had to close the shop for a day while I apologized to Alle and we cleaned up the mess, finishing by banning my aunt and cousins from the premises amid much pouting and protestations about my mean and ungrateful behavior.

But now I was packing for my journey to the Far Isles, where Luka and I would spend the next two months visiting with our dragon friends in their newfound haven. The only thing that dampened my anticipation was the look on Hagen's face. He seemed . . . jealous.

Or so I realized as I came out from under the bed with the errant stocking in hand. I looked at my brother as he poked morosely at a stack of shifts.

"Hagen," I said, inspiration dawning, "would you like to come with us?"

He looked up at me, his face glowing. He had grown so tall, and taken on so many responsibilities in the last few years, that it was hard to remember that he was my *younger* brother, and barely seventeen. "Could I really?"

"I don't see why not. The dragons have all heard about you: they are very grateful that you look after Theoradus's hoard, and I'm sure they would love to meet you."

Although the display rooms for Theoradus's hoard had been specifically designed to accommodate dragon as well as human visitors, the dragons had been banished from Feravel only days after its completion, and none of them had had a chance to visit.

"I can talk to a real live dragon?" His voice was awed. "And fly on its back?"

"Yes!" I gave him a quick hug. It would be wonderful to have my brother with me on the journey. "Pack your things; we'll be starting early tomorrow."

How early, I didn't even want to contemplate. The King's Seat was in the middle of Feravel. It was a week's ride to the border of Roulain, and another week's ride across Roulain to the ocean. A ship would carry us two days' journey out, and leave us on a tiny, uninhabited island called Black Gull Rock, where Shardas and Feniul would meet us.

"If dragons were allowed in human lands we wouldn't have to do this," I grumbled to Luka early the next morning as I loaded my luggage onto the backs of the patient packhorses.

"I know, I know," he said soothingly. "Give my father time. I'm sure he'll let a few dragons come and go . . . in a while."

With a snort, I picked up the last basket of clothing and handed it to a groom, who carefully strapped it to the back of the packhorse. The horse looked bored, and lowered its head as though thinking about taking a nap until it was time to leave. I could hardly blame it: dawn hadn't come yet, and a moment before I had yawned until my jaw popped unpleasantly.

Alle staggered to the door of the shop, still in her dressing gown and with her hair mussed. She yawned, and I popped my jaw again, copying her.

"You shouldn't have gotten up," I told her. "You're going to have a busy day: Luka just told me that the invitations to the Autumn Masquerade were sent yesterday."

She rolled her eyes. "And don't tell me that you're not secretly thrilled to get out of making an exotic bird costume for some wealthy dowager with four chins and an enormous . . ." She saw Luka and blushed. "Your Highness," she squeaked, "I didn't mean . . . of course not all the wealthies . . ."

"Creel's thrilled," Luka said, smiling brightly. "But not because of your clients. It's because if we stay here, she'll be invited to attend the masquerade, and then *she'll* have to dress up like an exotic bird or a flower and try to dance with spangles and fringy things all over her."

Alle giggled. Then she walked over to poke at the baskets of luggage. "You haven't forgotten your gown, have you? You know which one?" She gave Luka a sly glance.

"Which gown is that?" Luka looked all innocence.

"The one you're not supposed to see," I teased him. I pointed to the last basket. "It's in there," I told Alle. "I've got all the material, thread, beads, buttons, and lace I could possibly ever need. So don't worry: it will be done by the time we return, and you and Marta won't have to scramble to finish my wedding gown the week before the wedding."

"Just don't drop it in the ocean or let a dragon scorch it," she said, rubbing her hands together in the cold morning air. "Or lose it. Or let it drag in the dirt. Or—"

"Alle!" I took her shoulders and gave her a little shake. "I have handled fine fabrics before, you know!"

She gave me a dire look. "Your history with fine gowns isn't as perfect as you think. Remember *The Gown?*"

Only one of my creations was referred to in that way. It was a golden gown, re-made from the castoffs of a horrible princess. I had worn it to the Merchants' Ball, where I had first revealed my plan to open my own dress shop. That night, Shardas, my beloved dragon friend, had been forced to attack the New Palace in the battle that began the First Dragon War. The second time I had worn the gown—cleaned and with the damaged parts replaced—Shardas had accidentally yanked the window out of the Royal Chapel and nearly put a complete stop to Miles and Isla's wedding. After that, the gown was largely held to be cursed, which was why I hadn't told Marta or Alle that I was taking it with me to the Far Isles.

I was going to donate it to the hoard of a dragon named Gala, a friend from the Second Dragon War, who loved fine sewing and whose hoard had been taken away from her years ago, when Shardas's cruel brother, Krashath, had enslaved her. The fact that this gown was in my luggage was a secret, though, in case Luka or one of the guards recognized it and did something foolish out of fear of some silly curse.

A gown could not be cursed! At least, I didn't think so.

After giving Alle a hug, and telling her to keep an eye on the new apprentices and to give Marta another hug from me, I mounted up. I had half-hoped that Marta and Tobin would come to see us off since their little house was only a few streets away, but it was very early, and quite cold, so I could hardly blame them for staying home.

Our horses' hooves clattered on the cobblestones as we set off down the street. Luka and Hagen and I rode in the front, Hagen looking like he was going to nod off and fall right out of the saddle. Behind us came guards and grooms and the string of pack animals.

Normally when Luka went on a journey, he started from the New Palace, in full daylight, with people there to cheer and wave, and his father making a speech about how proud he was of Luka and giving him a royal kiss on each cheek. But King Caxel didn't approve of this journey, and my association with the dragons still made some people wary, so we started out in darkness and alone but for the few servants who had agreed to accompany us.

As we passed the street where Marta lived, someone called my name. I glanced over, and there was Marta, still in her night robe, running toward us on bare feet. "Creel! Creel!" Tobin was right behind her, fully dressed, but looking groggy. Marta caught my horse's bridle with a gasp. "Sorry! Overslept!"

I dismounted and gave her a hug. "It's all right. Now get inside before you catch your death!" I gave Tobin a hug as well. Hagen and Luka had also dismounted, and now they hugged Marta, and punched Tobin's shoulders in a manly way. We promised to bring them gifts, and Marta promised to keep the shop running smoothly.

And then, of course, she reminded me to take care of my wedding gown.

"Honestly!" I shook my head as a snickering Luka helped me back onto my horse. "It will be fine! I will return with a gorgeous, *clean*, finished gown, Marta!"

"See that you do," she said severely.

Waving, we started out for the second time. Hagen was more awake now, and was asking one of the guards about his duties and whether or not he had ever fought in a battle. Luka was still looking at me with an amused expression.

"What?" I knew I sounded irritable, but it was too early in the morning for me to be more pleasant. Usually I would sleep for another two hours, then have a leisurely breakfast while I sorted through the day's work.

"What will you do if something does go wrong with the wedding gown?" His eyes twinkled.

I stuck out my tongue. "I suppose I shall just have to postpone our wedding until I have made a new one. You wouldn't mind waiting another year, would you?" I smiled sweetly and tapped my horse with my heels, moving ahead of him. "After all: you wouldn't want me to get married in a badly made gown!"

Luka shook his head, chuckling, and heeled his own horse up beside mine. "No," he said, "I wouldn't want that."

Beyond the Horizon

This really *is* just a big rock," Hagen said, kicking at it.
Black Gull Rock was rough and dark and resembled
a large stone haystack sitting on a platter. It was not really
even large enough to be called an island—in point of fact it
was barely bigger than my bedchamber, and far more precar-
ious to walk around—and the thought of being left on it was
making me increasingly nervous. I wiped my sweaty palms
on my tunic and watched the men unloading the longboat
closely. The waves caused the boat to bob up and down, and
several times the men were in danger of either smashing the
hull into the rock or dropping our luggage into the water.

Some little ways off, the ship that had brought us here was
anchored, the crew gathered on the rails to watch. Whether
they were waiting for a rogue wave to sweep us into the
ocean or eager to see a dragon up close, I didn't know, but
their scrutiny was making me more self-conscious.

What if Shardas didn't come? What if the clouds on the
horizon were a storm that would send us all to our deaths?

Luka put his arms around me. "Stop worrying," he said.
"Shardas will be here."

Just then Hagen leaped forward and grabbed a basket

from one of the men before it plunged into the water. The sailor who had been passing it over looked chagrined, and muttered a "thanks" that was lost in the crash of the waves. When I saw which basket it was, my heart did a little flip. I snatched it from my brother and held it to my chest awkwardly, since it was the size of a barrel and I couldn't fit my arms around it.

Hagen's eyes widened. "Is that your wedding gown?"

"Yes!" I clutched it tighter. I should have lined the inside of the basket with oilskin, but I had been more concerned about running out of thread, and hadn't thought about what to do if the basket fell into the ocean.

Shouting from the ship caught our attention, and we looked to see the sailors waving their caps and pointing at the sky. Those in the longboat now began frantically rowing back to the ship, looking less thrilled than their fellows. A shadow darkened the sky, and I looked up to see three dragons circling overhead: gold, green, and scarlet.

I set my basket down and waved to them, cheering and shouting greetings, and Luka joined me. Hagen gave a tentative wave, and looked pale. I shot him a grin, and went on waving to my friends as they settled in the water like stately ships.

Feniul, green as grass from his nose down to the tips of his claws, immediately began to talk. "Creel! So marvelous! Here we are! You remember Ria? My mate, Ria?"

The scarlet dragon, Ria, bobbed in the water and nodded to me. "Hello, my dear."

"Hello, Feniul! Hello, Ria!" I turned to the largest dragon, the gold dragon with his sapphire horns and gleaming blue eyes. "Hello, Shardas!"

"Creel," he said in his huge voice. "It is so good to see you in person once more." For the past year we had been talking through pools of water, which the dragons could transform into a mode of communication.

I couldn't stop laughing with delight at seeing my friends. "This is my brother, Hagen!" I yanked his arm until he came forward and bowed awkwardly. The dragons were genuinely pleased to meet him, and Shardas's praise for Hagen's careful keeping of Theoradus's hoard made my brother's ears turn pink.

Feniul was absolutely bursting with news: he and Ria had had seven hatchlings, which I knew, but as a proud father he wanted to tell me about each of them and their most recent accomplishments. He described their home to me, and hinted that there were surprises I could never imagine waiting on the Far Isles.

Before I could winkle the surprises out of Feniul, Shardas turned and looked over at the lowering clouds. "We should go, quickly."

Shardas and Feniul gripped the edge of the rock and we scrambled over their shoulders to fasten our luggage to the sharp spines running down their backs. Luka and Hagen climbed onto Ria, but Shardas indicated that I should mount him, just between the basket that held my wedding gown and the one that contained the sealed buckets of black sand.

"We have a great deal to talk about," Shardas said.

I blew Luka a kiss before Ria took off, kicking seawater at

me with her hind legs; then I clambered onto Shardas, hooting with joy at the thrill of flying again as he shot into the air. We circled the ship once, waving and calling down to the sailors, then headed south and east, toward the previously uninhabited islands that the dragons had claimed for their own.

"How far away are they?" I squinted, wondering how soon I would be able to see the Far Isles. There was nothing but blue water in every direction, and the ocean winds made the dragons soar at great speed.

Shardas's laugh vibrated my entire body. "Farther than you can see. Well beyond the horizon."

"Oh." I settled back, disappointed.

"Don't worry," he assured me. "It is worth the journey."

Whatever reply I might have made was whipped from my lips as the dragons surged forward, toward the edge of the world where the sky and the waves met, and beyond.

The Far Isles

After four days of flying, stopping only at night to eat and sleep on bleak islets not much larger than Black Gull Rock, we at last reached the Far Isles. No humans lived there, because the outer ring of islands were rough and inhospitable. Waves crashed against jagged rocks where only a few strands of sea grass grew and nothing but ornery-looking gulls ever took up residence. Because of the tides it was possible for ships to anchor there only a few months out of the year, Shardas told me. And he had never heard of anyone attempting the dangerous passage beyond the outer ring of tightly grouped islands. No one believed there was anything there worth the risk to discover.

This was what made the dragons' new home so safe. We, however, didn't have to anchor on the jagged shore; we simply flew over the barren mountains to the paradise beyond. Hidden by their ugly cousins was an inner ring of islands, the sight of which took my breath away.

The passage between the outer and inner islands softened the ocean break so that the water washed with gentle blueness on the white sand of the inner islands. Amidst the blue waters, like many-colored jewels, were the true Far Isles, as beautiful and welcoming as Shardas had described them. I squinted in the bright sunshine, taking in the vision before me and committing it to memory. I thought perhaps I might re-create it with cloth and embroidery silk, for it surely deserved such a tribute. I wondered, though, if I would be able to find the subtle greens, of which there were nearly a dozen different shades among my threads, or match that particular combination of turquoise water and creamy white sands.

The dragons veered left, taking us toward the largest of the islands. A gentle mountain, green with life, sloped up on one side, and past the white beach the trees were so thick that nothing else could be seen.

Until the dragons started to appear. They swooped out of the clouds around us, they trailed out of the jungle, they burst from the waves and shot spouts of water into the air as Luka and I cried out delighted greetings to old friends. Much of the exuberance came from the young ones: both hatchlings born in the last year, and those just slightly older. They raced around us in circles and called out to their parents in excitement. As we came in to land on the beach, I realized I had tears running down my cheeks. Seeing so many dragons, safe and happy together, filled my heart until it spilled out in the form of happy tears.

Luka understood, and when he climbed down from Ria and saw my wet face he gave me a tight hug. Shardas and Ria snorted their hot breath at me, their eyes bright with shared emotion.

Feniul just dithered.

"We were planning on only two human guests, of course . . . not that you aren't more than welcome, Hagen. But you'll have to share a hut with Luka, and it is rather small. Just temporary, you know, but still . . ."

"Feniul," his mate said with infinite patience, "why don't you round up our hatchlings to introduce them?"

And so we were introduced to Feniul and Ria's hatchlings, all green and red and yellow, and absolutely full of energy. We were greeted by Amacarin, the second dragon I had ever exchanged words with, and his mate, Gala. Amacarin had been the particular friend of Theoradus of Carlieff, but he and I were on good terms despite his initial desire to help Theo-radus roast and eat me.

Gala, who had been freed from the Citatian army the year before, had several almost-grown hatchlings, and was proud to report that in a few weeks' time she and Amacarin would cel-ebrate the hatching of a fine batch of six eggs. I congratulated them sincerely; the dragons of Feravel had been so isolated that I knew Amacarin had despaired of ever finding a mate, let alone siring children.

Stately, green Niva with her alchemist mate, Leontes, and their children came forward next. She had been an ally since the First Dragon War, a staunch supporter of Shardas and Velika, and had risked capture to help us spy on the Citatians during the second war. I had never met her mate before, though. He was the same size as she, with striking yellow and violet scales and a twinkling good humor in his eyes, at odds with his mate's often severe nature.

Then came Darrym, another dragon we had rescued from

the Citatian army. He was an anomaly here: next to his peacock-bright and cottage-sized fellows, Darrym was perhaps the size of a large hay cart, and a muddy brown and green color that made his scales look dull and perpetually dirty. I didn't know where he was from, and my limited knowledge of geography made it rather useless for me to ask, but I wondered now if he were the product of Krashath's horrid breeding program, which had been formed in an effort to swell the ranks of the Citatian army as rapidly as possible.

Bobbing up and down in front of me, Darrym seemed distracted, and asked twice if I had seen Velika yet. I shared his distraction. I, too, was anxious about Shardas's beloved mate.

"No, no, I haven't," I told him.

Velika had not had an easy life, though she was strong. She had befriended King Milun the First hundreds of years ago, only to be betrayed by him. He had cut the skin from her breast to make a pair of slippers that could control any dragons within a thousand leagues, and trapped her in the caverns beneath the King's Seat. She had emerged from that prison only to dive into the Boiling Sea to destroy the slippers.

Badly burned himself, Shardas had cared for her in hiding until his brother, Krashath, had threatened us all by raising an army of dragons. What Krashath had wanted was Velika herself, who, as the queen of the dragons, was the key to ruling them all.

"Creel, Luka, Hagen: she is coming," Shardas said now, his voice brimming with an emotion that I couldn't place. He turned and looked toward the jungle, and I saw a dragon-sized path cut through the trees.

"This is the big surprise!" Feniul convulsively lashed his tail, picking up his smallest daughter and flinging her high in the air. She did a flip, squealing with glee, and landed on his back.

Sapphire blue, with gleaming silver gray horns, Velika emerged from the jungle at a strangely slow and halting pace. My heart lurched—had she been injured? What had happened?

But her eyes glowed, and so did Shardas's, as she came to stand beside him. She lowered her long muzzle, and I rested one hand lightly between her eyes.

"Are you? I mean, what's . . . er . . ." My words stumbled as I caught sight of her bulging belly. Eggs!

Shardas let out a bellow of laughter. "The hatching will not be for some time after, but I think you will be here when our eggs are laid." The emotion in his voice was pride and joy, and several of the dragons around us let out bellows of their own.

My eyes brimmed with tears again, and I ducked under Velika's chin to hug her neck. It was a liberty I never would have dared take just last year, but I couldn't help myself. Hatchlings, after all this time!

Seeing the little stone huts where we were to live and the evening feast on the shore were just a blur after that. It wasn't until later, sitting on a log by the bonfire with Luka, that I could even string more than two words together.

"This is all so wonderful," I said, sighing.

"It's the most amazing thing that's ever happened to me," Hagen chimed in. He was holding out a long stick with a piece of yellow fruit on the end. Riss, one of Gala's daughters, was toasting the fruit for him with a small tendril of blue dragonfire.

Darrym came up, still bobbing his head around awkwardly. But then, I didn't really know him all that well, and the last time we had spoken had been in the aftermath of a war. "So, you, ah, didn't know about Velika at all?" he said.

"Not a hint of it," I told him. "Isn't it thrilling?"

"Yes," he said. And now he added running sand compulsively between his foreclaws to his head bobbing. "It's more than we could have hoped for. First to find the queen alive, and then for her to have children . . ." More bobbing. "Yes, it's more than we could have hoped!" He went off into the jungle.

"What under the Triunity is he talking about?" I turned to Riss for an explanation but she just shook her head in confusion.

"I don't remember him being quite so Feniul-like before," Luka said after the green and brown dragon had disappeared into the trees.

"Isn't he one of the ones who was collared? In Citatie?" Hagen blew on his roasted fruit before popping it into his mouth. "That would make anyone behave strangely," he said, talking around a mouthful of hot fruit.

"Very true," Luka agreed.

"No, he's just strange." Riss snickered. "He doesn't have a hoard." She said this as though it sealed the matter in stone.

"I didn't think any of you had hoards, at least not yet," Luka said.

That reminded me that we had not yet presented Shardas with the black sand, or the other items we had brought as gifts. He had gone to escort Velika to her bed; she tired easily this close to laying her eggs.

"We have *some* things," Riss said defensively. "But he doesn't want anything."

"Perhaps he was born into the collar and doesn't have the instinct," I said thoughtfully. "How would he know what he liked? He wouldn't even have heard of a hoard until just last year."

Riss shrugged. "Strange."

Amacarin came then to tell her to go to bed, and Feniul and Niva settled in to hear the news from Feravel, so I pushed any thought of Darrym to the back of my mind.

And tomorrow there would be gifts, and an entire island to explore.

Rebuilding the Hoards

Y ou're sure?" Gala stared at the gold gown with awe.

"Yes, please," I said fervently. "If you don't take it, I think one of my apprentices might burn it. Both times I've worn it something bad has happened, and she told me that she sometimes has trouble sleeping, just knowing that it's in my wardrobe across the hall."

Gala shook her head. "A very odd human." She delicately lifted the stiff overskirt with a claw, studying the blue silk underneath. "So lovely! And how did you know that fancy-work was my passion?"

"I asked Velika if there was anything I could bring with me, to help you all get settled," I told her. "And, because I'm a dressmaker, she knew that I would have something for you."

"The queen is ever thoughtful," Gala said. "And this is particularly exquisite." She closely studied the embroidery of the bodice.

"It is some of my best work," I said, trying and failing to sound modest. "So I'm glad that it will have someone to admire it."

I had brought a collapsible dressmaker's dummy with me as well, and now the golden gown hung from the wicker frame, the rich fabric glowing softly in the torchlight that lit Gala and Amacarin's cave. Gala settled down beside the gown, arranging herself over the sandy nest of eggs as though prepared to admire the gown all day while she warmed her babies. I went out into the sunshine with her mate.

"Thank you, Creel," Amacarin said sincerely. He and I had never exactly been friends, but Gala and her children seemed to have had a softening effect on him. "It will do her good to begin collecting again."

"And what about you?" I looked up at him, hiding a smile. I had something for Amacarin in the bag slung over my shoulder; I just hadn't told him yet.

"Oh, I was able to return to my cave in Feravel when the exile began, and retrieve a few things," he said, but he gazed into the distance as though thinking of all the items he hadn't retrieved. "I suppose the rest was taken away by humans. I can only hope they know how to care for fine vellum properly." He made a swiping gesture, as though wiping invisible dust off his own foreleg.

"Luka's brother, Prince Miles, gathered your books up personally," I told him, still trying to hide a smile. "He has added them to the royal library, where they will be very well looked after."

"That's good, I suppose," he said, his voice distant.

"Unfortunately, one or two items have gone missing recently," I said, unable to contain myself any longer. I reached into the bag and pulled out two rare scrolls of lyric poetry from the fifth century. The scrolls had taken up so little room, Luka had had to stop me from stealing more. I handed them to

Amacarin, who cradled them in his claws as if they were babies.

"Oh, Creel!" His voice was reverent. "The works of Malester Punin? Thank you!" He lowered his muzzle and inhaled the scent of dust and parchment. "Thank you! I must . . . Gala will . . ."

"Go and show her." I laughed.

He turned and went back into the cave, calling out to his new mate. "Only see, Gala! See what our lovely human friend brought me!"

Smiling, I walked back down to the beach. Luka and Shardas were waiting for me by a large oven that Shardas had made from sheets of iron. I had seen the clay ovens the dragons used to bake huge slabs of moist, spongy, berry bread, but I had no idea what this big, black oven was for.

"Where'd you get the iron?" Hagen was walking around the contraption, kicking it in that knowledgeable way that boys have.

"I traded for it in Moralien," Shardas said. Moralien was the one country that hadn't shut the dragons out entirely. The Moralienin had always been explorers and traders and would trade with a human, dragon, or talking dog if there were rare goods to be had.

"What did you trade?" Hagen looked curiously at Shardas. "I thought you didn't have any—" He colored. "I mean, I didn't think dragons . . ."

"Have money? No, we don't. I captured some exotic birds here on the island, and used them to barter," Shardas said, chuckling.

I gave him a worried look. "I thought you weren't going to trade anything too interesting for a while," I reminded him. "So that people won't guess that the Far Isles aren't barren and horrid."

Shardas looked sheepish. "I said that I had found them flying somewhere off the coast of a country I couldn't remember," he said. "I *think* they believed me."

"I certainly hope so."

Luka shook his head and indicated the buckets at his feet. "If you are quite finished scolding the king of the dragons, Creel, we do have a gift for him."

Now my cheeks were red, and Hagen was smirking at me. I hadn't meant to scold. I hid my embarrassment by going to stand beside Luka as he picked up one of the covered buckets and presented it to Shardas.

"Er, thank you," Shardas said, taking the bucket with a puzzled look. Then he lifted the lid. "Black sand!"

"Black sand?" Velika had lumbered up in her stately yet cumbersome way. "What is it for?"

"It melts into a fine red glass," Shardas told her with delight. "I shall make you a scarlet vase." He looked down at Luka and me. "Thank you so very much!"

"Luka found it on some secluded beach in Moralien," I said, squeezing my betrothed's waist. "I wouldn't have known it was different from any other sand," I admitted.

"It's hard to see how something like this could change into red glass," Shardas agreed, running a claw through the coarse, dark grains. He carefully poured some of the sand into an iron pan and set it in the oven.

"Do you use these to shape the glass?" Hagen picked up a long tube lying by the base of the oven.

"Does everyone in this world know how to make glass except me?" I huffed.

"Barten Foss is a glassmaker," Hagen said with a shrug.

"Barten Foss? That horrible, gangly boy who used to call me 'Spotty'?" I wrinkled my nose.

"I wouldn't call him horrible or gangly around our cousin Leesel," Hagen said. "They're courting." Then it was his turn to look embarrassed suddenly. "Although, Aunt Reena told her not to get too attached. She's planning on arranging marriages for Leesel and Pella to any nobles caught unawares in the palace."

Luka laughed until his eyes watered. "I almost wish we were back at the palace to witness that," he said when he could speak.

I hid my mortification by trying to peer into the oven. "So the sand will melt?"

"Yes," Shardas said, taking pity on me and tapping the pan with a claw. I had to shield my eyes as the fire crackled and the heat made sweat break out across my forehead and down my neck. "When it becomes the consistency of soft toffee, it is ready to be shaped."

"Have you had much success so far?" I had to step away from the oven, and Velika obligingly coiled her tail so that I could sit on it. The heat had quite taken my breath away.

At least Luka had the sense to stay well clear of the fire. Hagen, though, was still caught up in studying the metal tubes and the exterior of the oven.

"Well," Shardas said slowly, "the glass is certainly clear." He ducked his head and scuffed at the sand around our feet.

"I'm sure that with practice your creations will be more regular in shape," Velika said reassuringly.

"More regular in shape?" I arched an eyebrow.

"Less lopsided," Shardas admitted. "And less lumpy."

I laughed, but not to be rude. "You should have seen my first embroidery samplers. Awful!"

"You see, my dear," Velika said, "if you want to do anything well, you must practice."

Tapping the pan again, Shardas gave a sulfurous sigh. "I know. But I shall make you a vase from this sand, Velika, and it will not be lopsided."

"I'd still like to see what you've done so far," I said. "I haven't seen your cave yet." But then the oven made a hissing sound and my attention was drawn back to our current experiment.

"Almost ready," Shardas said. He blew a single thin tendril of blue flame into the oven, and the hissing turned to a bubbling. "Stand back."

Luka and Hagen lined up beside Velika and me, away from the oven and the long pipes. Hagen's face was wistful, and I knew that he longed to stand right beside Shardas, maybe even hold one of the pipes. I sympathized, but at the same time, I did not want to see my little brother get burned. I took his hand and he gave me a brief smile before both of us turned back to Shardas.

Having selected one of the pipes—a gleaming shaft about double my height but not quite big enough around for me to put my arm into—Shardas gently set the end of it in the pan of melted sand and rolled it. We watched as a glob of a glowing red, taffy-like substance stuck to the end. When it was big enough to suit him, Shardas pulled it out of the oven. He continued to roll the pipe as he gently blew into one end.

The candylike red blob on the other end of the pipe began to swell. It grew larger and rounder, more transparent, like a soap bubble that was about to burst. I found that I was holding my breath, willing it not to pop, as the red liquid glass grew to the size of my head, then of a large melon.

Shardas twirled the pipe as he blew, a few times slowly, then fast. There was a large block of polished marble beside the oven and he gently rested part of the blob on it, still twirling. The glass connected to the pipe contracted, and the shape of a vase clearly emerged. Shardas lifted the pipe to give it one more twirl, still blowing through the end, and one of the sides of the vase began to bulge out.

"Uh-oh," Hagen whispered.

Not to be daunted by the now decidedly lopsided shape of his project, Shardas reached out with one foreclaw and cut the glass loose from the pipe, setting it gently on the block. Working quickly, he scratched and pulled and prodded at the glass with his claws fully extended, while we all leaned in a little bit to see what he was doing. He was panting now, from both the heat and the urgency of his movements, as it was plain that the glass was cooling rapidly.

Shardas pulled the lip of the vase wide, but it was sitting atop too thin a neck, and I gripped Hagen's hand even more tightly as the top of the vase slowly collapsed. We all groaned as one, and Shardas slumped over his creation as it cooled and hardened. Gleaming, finely etched by his diamond-hard claws, but flawed and lopsided and . . .

"Perfect," Velika said softly.

Her mate raised his head.

"Only see how the shape reminds one of a tightly closed trumpet flower," she went on. "And the color, magnificent! The light sparks off it, and the etching draws the eye around the asymmetrical base perfectly."

I could tell from her voice that she wasn't just humoring Shardas, and so could he. She sounded like any collector viewing a fine piece for the first time. Shardas's blue eyes locked with those of his mate.

"It won't hold flowers," Hagen said reverently. "But it's still brilliant! A work of art, created by a dragon!"

If a dragon could blush, Shardas would have. "I'll keep practicing," he muttered. "And I should save the rest of this black sand until I improve."

"And I keep telling him that he needs no improvement," Velika said. "As Hagen said, it won't hold flowers, but it is still brilliant! The jungle around us is full of flowers, Shardas; I don't need vases to put them in. I simply enjoy looking at your glass pieces as works of art." She extended her long neck, and touched her nose to Shardas's. "When this piece cools, it will make a fine addition to my hoard."

"I'd love to see the rest of Shardas's work," I said. I hated to break up the tender moment, but the combination of the tropical sun and the heat of the glassblowing ovens was making me sweat like a prize hog on butchering day, to borrow a phrase of Hagen's. "Your cave must be nice and cool right now," I hinted.

"Ah, yes! Forgive me," Shardas said. "I often forget how hot the ovens can be, especially at midday."

"The orchards are also nice and cool," Velika said pointedly. "And young Master Carlbrun is accounted an expert in such things. At least according to his sister."

Now it was Hagen's turn to blush, while Luka and I elbowed him in the ribs.

With a rumble of laughter, Shardas looked at Hagen. "*Would* you be so kind as to look at our orchard before we retire to our cave for refreshment? I am worried that the trees are not growing as straight as they should."

"Don't you have them staked?" Hagen's blushes faded, and his tone was immediately businesslike.

"I've been wanting to see the orchards myself," Luka put in. "Personally, I'm curious to see how soil this sandy can hold up any kind of tree."

"It's a different soil inland," Shardas said, banking the oven and setting the glassblowing pipe carefully aside. "Thick, red soil, from the volcanoes that formed the islands."

"While you go kick the red dirt around in the orchards," Velika said, "I believe that I shall go and take a nap!"

She led the way up the path into the jungle until it forked. Then we all waved as she went off to the left, to the cave she shared with Shardas (which I was still dying to see). We continued on to the right, however, toward the orchards of the dragons.

Peach Trees and Honey Squash

"Are these the birds that you traded to the Moralienin?" I ducked as another red and blue plumed nuisance dove across the path and nearly grazed my head.

"Yes. There are also smaller green ones," he said. Then he shook his head vigorously as one of the red-and-blues tried to land on his horns.

"They're more annoying than Marta's monkey," Luka said, waving both hands over his head to keep them away.

The birds screeched and continued to dive at us. One of them settled on a nearby branch and began berating us. I stopped in my tracks, however, when it actually called out, "Stupid creatures!"

"Can they talk?"

"Yes," Shardas said curtly, "making them even worse than Marta's monkey. If you talk to them, they will mimic the words. Unfortunately, most of what they hear are curse words, so please don't be shocked if they call you ruder things than 'stupid.'"

We all laughed at that, and I asked about Marta's monkey, Ruli. She had bought it in Citatie, but the horrid little thing had taken a shine to Feniul's mate, Ria, and had come to the Far Isles with them. I had been quite relieved, for the tiny black-and-white animal was fond of shredding silk, and the thought of it getting loose in our shop had filled me with terror.

"Oh, you haven't seen him yet? He's around here some-where," Shardas assured me. "Velika finds Ruli particularly trying, though, so I believe that Ria is keeping him well away from us. And, by the First Fires, I can't say that I miss him!"

The path forked again, sweeping away to our left and our right, and Shardas stopped and pointed at the trees straight ahead. "Here they are," he said.

"Here are what?"

But as I came around Shardas's massive, golden haunches I saw that the trees in front of us weren't the usual jungle trees with their frothy leaves atop tall branchless trunks. These were ordinary Feravelan trees, peach and apricot, and I thought I saw apple to one side. They appeared to be nearly as tall as the jungle trees because they were planted on huge mounds of red dirt, and were in clusters rather than the straight lines of an orchard.

"It's, er, rather an unusual orchard," Luka said, giving voice to my thoughts.

We walked a little ways to the left, and saw other mounds, with paths winding between them. Some of them had trees planted on them; others had melon vines, or beanstalks care-fully staked upright. The reasoning behind these circular gar-den plots finally struck me, and I shook my head at my own foolishness.

"Of course," I said aloud. "If you planted the trees in rows a few paces apart, the way we humans do . . ."

"They would be too close together for us dragons to care for," Shardas finished.

"And the mounds probably help with irrigation," Hagen said knowledgeably.

He was already moving toward the foremost group of trees, nodding his head in a wise fashion. It was still strange to me to see how much my little brother had changed in the past three years.

Hagen had a keen mind, and had sat at the head of his age group in our tiny school in Carlieff. He had been a hard worker on our farm and then our uncle's, after our mother and father had died. Which is why Hagen had not been considered a burden by our aunt, and so she had kept him, while sending me off to be eaten by a dragon.

After the First Dragon War, when I had volunteered Hagen as caretaker of the display of Theoradus's hoard, he had risen to the honor with distinction. Or so I had been told by the Duke of Mordrel, who had been sent to make the initial arrangements. The Duke had been the first to tell me that my brother had begun cultivating the land just to the south of Theoradus's cave. Despite our family's previously unsuccessful attempts at farming, Hagen's peaches flourished, as did his plums and his grapes, and I could only gape when crates of preserves arrived at my shop, accompanied by Hagen's cheery notes about how many visitors Theoradus's hoard of shoes had had that season, or how many swains our girl cousins had collected, plus a good deal of bragging about how he had at last found the crops that our family was meant to farm.

But it didn't end with simply growing fruit. Hagen was fascinated by where different plants came from and what their uses were. He no longer allowed his plums to be made into preserves or dried, but sold the entire crop to an alchemist who made cough medicine with them. The alchemist had also helped Hagen with several experiments involving crossbreeding grapes and cherries, something I didn't understand, but freely bragged about.

And now it seemed that the bragging had been justified. As I watched, Hagen moved from tree to tree, pulling at branches, plucking leaves and studying them. He kicked at the soil, even bent down and raked his fingers through it, and squinted at the little ditches that I could only assume carried water between the trees and around the mounds.

"These trees will need to be staked, or they're going to grow crooked," Hagen told Shardas. "And this soil feels too heavy. Do you mulch?"

"Er . . ." Shardas scratched at the red dirt with his foreclaws. Then he raised his head and bellowed, "Roginet!"

I took a step backward. I had been standing rather close, and Shardas's bellow blew my hair back from my face. "Oof!"

"Sorry," Shardas rumbled.

"What's Roginet?" Hagen looked eager. "Some sort of fertilizer?"

"I am not a fertilizer," said a faintly accented voice. An orange dragon I had never seen before came from behind one of the other mounds and bowed to Shardas. "I am, however, a gardener." He said this as grandly as if announcing that he was a duke or prince.

"Roginet is in charge of our orchards and gardens," Shardas explained. "He has a passion for growing things."

"It 'as been some years since I was able to plant on such a large scale, 'owever," Roginet explained. "And I used to plant only ze cherry trees."

"Roulaini," Luka said out of the corner of his mouth.

I nodded slightly, having just recognized the accent myself. The Roulaini dragons had also gone into hiding after Milun the First had betrayed Velika, and had only come out into the open when Shardas had called for them to help fight Citatie during the Second Dragon War.

"This is young Hagen Carlbrun," Shardas said. "And you have no doubt heard of his sister, Creel, and her betrothed, Prince Luka of Feravel."

"Ah, yes!" Roginet bowed to the three of us. "I 'ave seen you both from afar," he said.

"Young Hagen was just advising me to stake these trees so that they grow straighter," Shardas said.

"Ah, me! I had forgotten ze staking," Roginet said to Hagen. "Thank you."

"You—you're welcome." Hagen was still uncomfortable being consulted by dragons, I could tell.

"And he mentioned *mulch*," Shardas said. He said the last word as if it were completely foreign to him.

"Ah, ze mulching!" Roginet nodded enthusiastically. "I 'ave been using our own waste, but do you zink it is too 'eavy?"

Shardas immediately stopped running the soil through his claws. "You've been using what?"

"Mulch is usually a mixture of dung and some other things, leaves maybe," Hagen explained.

Luka, too, drew back from the mound, while I just laughed. Having grown up on a farm, I knew exactly what mulch was.

"Do you zink zat our mulch is too strong?" Roginet fingered the soil, bending his head to Hagen's.

"You might want to try a bird-dropping-based mulch," Hagen mused. "I use turkey droppings."

"We 'ave not the turkeys here," Roginet said. "But there are many other birds."

Farm girl or not, this was about as much discussion of mulch as I could stand, and so I took Luka's arm and we strolled farther down the path. The mounds of trees gave way to clusters of grape vines strung on wires, vines on the ground bearing melons, and vegetable plots. Shardas soon joined us, and we went to select some honey melons from one of the mounds to eat with our dinner.

"It seems that you're doing very well here, sir," Luka said as he and I climbed among the vines, knocking on the sides of the round, yellow fruits.

"Indeed, we could not have asked for a better land to settle," Shardas agreed. "The climate is mild year 'round, so we are able to keep our gardens growing constantly. A good thing, considering how much food a single dragon can eat in a year. And we have taken pains not to farm any of the areas where wild fruits and animals flourish."

"What kind of animals live here, other than those screeching birds?" I pulled out my belt knife and cut the vine from one of the melons I had chosen.

"Oh, wild pigs, some strange little things that look like tiny bears—not very good eating, but they have to be kept away from the gardens or they tear them all to bits. Oh, and goats. Quite delightful little creatures, really. Different from Feravelan goats, and their milk and cheese are sweeter. Would you like to see the goat herds?"

Our nearest neighbors when I was a child had had goats. I remembered the smell, and the bruises I got when one of the males decided he didn't like me. I smiled politely at Shardas and declined.

"Delightful little goats?" Luka chuckled. "You know, sir, you and my father are two vastly different kings. Well, I don't think he knows what mulch is either, but I cannot imagine him even caring to find out. Let alone describing a herd of goats as 'delightful.'"

"Perhaps your father is missing out on some of life's small joys, then," Shardas offered. "These particular goats have a rather unusual habit of keeling over in a dead faint from excitement when they see strangers. And since they can barely remember who fed them breakfast an hour ago, they more or less think everyone is a stranger."

"They faint?" That got even my attention.

"They faint," Shardas said, laughing. "Come along and see, if you don't believe me."

We put the melons in a large net, and slung it under Shardas's belly. Then he flew Luka and me over the rest of their gardens and orchards, and yet more jungle, to a high, grassy plateau near the sea.

From his back, we watched the black and brown goats scatter in panic, and the moment his claws touched the ground, every last one of them had fallen over and was lying on its side, eyes rolled back and legs stiff. Luka and I had to sit right down on the short-cropped turf and hold our stomachs, we were laughing so hard.

There were tears streaming from my eyes, so I nearly missed seeing Darrym creep up over the edge of the cliff. I wiped my face on my sleeve, and watched him weave between some rocks as though trying to sneak away without us noticing him.

Shardas, however, was not teary-eyed from laughter, and from his height had an even better view of the brown and green dragon. He hailed Darrym, who froze before turning to face us.

"Hello, er, Shardas," Darrym said. "And . . . Creel and . . . Prince."

He bobbed up and down, displaying that strange tic we had noticed before. There was a bulky canvas sack hanging from his neck.

"I didn't think you had herding duty today," Shardas said.

"Oh, yes, I, er, volunteered. Miral was not feeling, er, well." More bobbing.

"Sorry to have made your charges faint," Shardas told him.

Darrym looked around in surprise, just now seeing the goats all lying about stiff. His tail came around and prodded one, which rolled over and began to snore, apparently over its initial terror.

"Do they do this often?" Darrym appeared mystified.

"Have you never had this duty before?" Shardas's voice had a slight edge to it now.

"I don't believe so." Darrym took off the sack and stashed it behind some rocks. With distaste he began to poke at more of the goats. Some of them leaped up and ran off, while others made themselves more comfortable and went to sleep.

"We shall leave you to it, then," Shardas said.

Luka and I scrambled back onto his neck, and the king of the dragons leaped into the air without so much as a good-bye for Darrym and his herd of strange charges. I thought this just a bit rude of Shardas, even considering Darrym's odd behavior. I said so as diplomatically as I could once we had returned to the gardens where we had left Hagen.

"He is rather grating on my nerves," Shardas admitted. "He seems to think himself above work of any kind, and I often catch him standing on the path near my cave for no reason."

"I wonder what was in that bag?" Luka said.

"I'm sure he was sitting on one of the cliff ledges, eating or reading and ignoring the goats," Shardas said, his voice dismissive. "And didn't want us to know."

"I suppose," Luka said, but he sounded doubtful.

I was doubtful as well. Darrym hadn't seen us until after he'd come up over the cliff lip, and there was no reason why someone assigned to sit and watch the goats all day couldn't be reading or eating while they did so. I wanted very much to know what was in that bag.

"You have to try some of this," Hagen said, running up to us with Roginet at his heels. Hagen thrust a bizarre, spiky fruit into my hands. "It grows wild here, and I've never tasted anything like it."

We all cut off sections of the fruit, which was shockingly tart but delicious, and then it was time to join Velika on the beach for supper. Soon, gorged on roasted pork and honey melons, I forgot all about Darrym.

The Palace of the Dragon King

A nd I will take Creel to our cave and show her some of your glass," Velika said.

"And then you should rest," Shardas reminded her.

"I will rest," she agreed.

We had been down at the beach most of the day, watching Shardas blow glass. Feniul and Ria had joined us, along with their hatchlings and various dogs, and we had watched the dragonlets and their pets run races and play in the water until they were all exhausted and lying in a heap in the shade of a giant palm tree.

The rest of us talked about the different animals that lived on the islands and how often the dragons could hope to export some of them—like the noisy birds—in exchange for the things they couldn't get here. Luka liked Shardas's story of having found the birds in the water after a storm had blown them from wherever their home might be, but Velika and I argued that there were only so many times that story could be used before people grew suspicious.

But now we were all feeling drowsy, and Shardas was urging his mate to return to their cave and have a nap. I had chimed in that I still hadn't seen their home, and would accompany her.

"I need to work on my gown anyway," I said. "I'll run by the hut and get it, and meet you farther up the path."

Velika moved so slowly that I didn't have to run at all to reach my little stone hut, gather up the basket with my wedding gown and sewing things, and meet her halfway to their home. She looked distinctly uncomfortable when I caught up to her, and paused in the shade of the jungle for a moment.

"The eggs will come soon," she assured me when I asked how she felt. "And then I shall feel much better. Afterward, Shardas and I must only take turns keeping them warm." Sighing, she led the way to their cave, which was right inside the central mountain.

It was different from Shardas's old cave, which had been formed from pale gray stone. The mountains of the Far Isles were long-dead volcanoes, and the rock was mostly rough and black and porous. To soften the floors, deep sand had been laid in the string of chambers, and I stopped to admire the pattern that claws and tails had made in the soft white sand. It would look good on a gown, I thought, and made a note to sketch it when I got the time.

Once again Shardas had used mirrors to reflect the light from small ventilation shafts, so the caves were well lit and full of fresh air. On a shelf carved out of the living rock was a row of strange, lumpy shapes.

Shardas's glassworks.

They were beautiful, and strange, I thought. If you had told me this one was a goblet, this other a plate, I would have laughed—they were too oddly shaped to be of actual use. But from a purely aesthetic stance . . .

"They truly are gorgeous," I breathed. With a reverent finger I traced the curve of one piece, stained faintly blue.

"I think so," Velika said, her voice soft. "I tease my mate because he will insist that they have a practical use, or that they will one day, at least. But I do enjoy looking upon them."

"Yes," I agreed. Studying the lines of a larger creation, this one translucent green and shaped vaguely like a tree, I saw how it might be meditative to gaze on them.

I lifted another green piece, this one no larger than a plum. It appeared to have started out as a flower, but then folded and collapsed in on itself. I held it up to the light, admiring the clarity of the glass and the complexity of its shape.

Laughing, Velika settled into the deep, sandy hollow at the side of the main cave.

"What is it?" I turned to look at her, still holding the lump of glass.

"You have picked your own gift out of the lot," she told me. "Shardas was making that for you. It was to be a flower. He almost threw it back in the furnace, but I told him to keep it anyway."

"Really?" The glass had a pleasing feel in my hand. "May I keep it then?"

"I think it is safe to say that you may."

Her eyelids drooped and I settled down by her side to sew while she napped, spreading my white gown out on a piece of coarse linen. I had all the pieces sewn together now: sleeves, bodice, collar, skirts, and was carefully stretching individual sections on my embroidery hoop and embroidering designs of dragons and trees and waves all over the gown. The designs were white on white, according to the tradition of the Triune Gods, but later I would sew on little crystals here and there—to highlight the dragons' eyes, the fruit on the trees—that would give it subtle flashes and sparkles of color.

We had used this technique on Marta's gown the year before. The idea had come from some silk we found in Citatie, which had tiny pieces of crystal or even metal sewn to it, creating a mirrored effect. We had used several lengths of the mirrored silk to create wing covers for Shardas, whose wings were still damaged from his dive into the Boiling Sea. The wing covers had enabled him to defeat his brother, the evil Krashath.

As magnificent as the wing covers had been, however, I was glad that we were only using mirrored silk and little crystals to make fine gowns now. I could live a long, full life, perfectly content, without ever having to see two dragons dueling again.

I kept the green glass flower where I could see it, and occasionally touch it, while I worked. It was very warm in the cave, and the silk of my gown was very soft. Before I knew it, I was asleep in a curve of Velika's tail.

A noise woke me, and I was disoriented when I opened my eyes. It was so dark in the cave that I knew it must be night. Only a few sparkles of bluish white light reflected off the mirrors. I peered around but didn't see Shardas. Velika was still

breathing deeply, profoundly asleep at my back. I wondered
how long we had been lying there, and why no one had come
to wake us yet.

Sticking my lumpy glass flower in the pocket of my tunic
and gathering my wedding gown into its basket so that it
wouldn't get stepped on, I stumbled out of the cave to look
for Luka and Shardas. There was a wide clearing at the
entrance, and in the light of the moons I could see Darrym
standing there. I wondered if he had been asked to stand
guard since Shardas wasn't here. It seemed odd, though, that
Velika would need a guard, and I opened my mouth to ask
him what he was doing. Was he just standing around staring,
the way Shardas had been talking about?

Then the humans, with their bows and arrows, came
creeping out of the jungle, and I shut my mouth.

At Moonrise

"Call the queen, Creel," Darrym said, his voice cold.

"No." I couldn't stop staring at the people surrounding me.

I had never seen people that looked like this, not even in the Grand Market, in the heart of cosmopolitan Pelletie.

They were all men, tall and nearly naked, covered in bizarre white tattoos and strings of dull beads. Their long hair was pulled back from their faces in weird topknots decorated with quills, and more quills had been sewn to the striped cloth that wrapped around their hips and thighs like bandages. The effect was both fascinating and intimidating.

And so were the arrows they were aiming at me.

"Call her," Darrym said again, his voice high and tense.

"Why? What are you doing? Who are these people?" My own voice sounded just as strange.

"Call her, or they will shoot," Darrym said.

One of the men did shoot, and the arrow buried itself in the sand directly between my feet. It was fletched with black feathers and the force of the shot had sunk it halfway into the sand.

"Velika!" I yelped. I couldn't help it, and stared at Darrym, still defiant. Velika was twice his size, and wooden arrows were no match for dragonfire.

"What is it?" It took her some time to come to the mouth of the cave, and her swollen belly caused her to half-skid out of the entrance before she had a chance to see the archers.

And then the net dropped over us.

It was made of stiff leather, and dripping with a greasy liquid that made my eyes water. Velika roared, and flamed, and clawed, but the net only tangled in her claws and her fire did nothing. The basket on my back pinned me to the ground, and I couldn't get my arms out of the straps.

The strange men yanked on ropes near their feet, and another net rose out of the sand where it had been concealed, trapping us like fish. Darrym rose into the air, taking some of the ropes in his claws, and two other small brown and green dragons came out of the trees to take the rest.

Velika and I were lifted up, awkwardly, frighteningly, in the nets and the dragons flew away with us. They barely cleared the trees, and I closed my eyes in terror, all the while screaming for someone to help us, but no friendly dragon appeared in the moonlight.

Silent except for an occasional moan, Velika was bunched beside and somewhat beneath me. Her scales were so hot it was making me uncomfortable. Once we were over the ocean and there was no one to hear my shouts but our kidnappers, I stopped yelling and tried to get her attention.

"Are you all right? Velika? I'm sorry, I didn't mean to call you, but the arrow . . ." My protest sounded weak and I fell silent. I could have stood up to Darrym, to them. I always said that I would do anything for my friends, but when the first arrow landed at my feet I betrayed them. I clenched my fingers around the strands of the net and mentally cursed my cowardice.

"It is all right, Creel," Velika said, her voice labored. "You could not have known . . . the other dragons . . . the fire-bane . . ."

"Firebane?"

"An herb . . . brews . . . a potion that can be used against dragons. Stops us from flaming, makes us sleep . . ."

In horror I realized that she meant the strange liquid on the net. It was extremely pungent; my nose and eyes streamed from the fumes. I began to yell again, my voice rough and strained, but this time I was yelling to our captors.

One in particular.

"Darrym! How could you do this to your queen?"

"It is because she is my queen," was the reply. "We need her."

Once again he had the brown canvas bag strung around his neck. What was inside it? Bottles of this firebane? A jar of alchemical water, used to bespeak his cohorts? I kicked out at the net in frustration, but only succeeded in entangling one of my feet in an awkward way.

"Who?" I practically screamed the question at him. "Who are these people? Where did these dragons come from?"

I had not seen every dragon in the world, but I knew that Darrym was considered unusual for his dull coloring and his pale, cowlike horns. Where had he met two other dragons who looked just like him? How long had they been planning this?

These questions went unanswered, however, as did any others I shouted to him. He would only tell me coolly that "they" needed Velika, and the firebane was a necessary evil. He patted the bag at his neck again. All his nervous bobbing, his obsequiousness was gone. In its place was a smug arrogance that made me wish I had some firebane to pour on *him*.

As dawn broke, I saw that we were encircled by eight dragons. Those who were not carrying the net clutched enormous wicker baskets. I could see the faces of the odd, stern warriors who had helped capture us peering over the edges as we flew south and east, far from Shardas and any hope of rescue.

The consoling thought that at least I was with Velika, to comfort and aid her, was soon dashed. A small rocky islet came into view, and Darrym gave the order to the group to fly low over it.

One of the dragons carrying a basket of warriors glided in close, and a man with a fierce grin and a golden spike piercing his nose leaned out and cut two of the strands of netting, nearly slicing my left arm in the process. He grabbed that arm, and my left knee, and gave a shout. His dragon flew even farther down, and I was pulled, screaming, through a hole in the net barely big enough to fit me. The basket containing my wedding gown stuck and nearly jerked my arms out of their sockets, but then it popped free as well. The man holding me leaned out over a bit of sand jutting away from the islet and let go.

I landed facedown, fortunately missing any rocks. By the time I had regained my wind and coughed out the sand I had swallowed, Darrym and Velika and the others were nearly out of sight. Velika hadn't been awakened by my struggles, and I worried anew for her and her eggs.

Tracking the flight as long as I could, I used a stick to mark their path in the sand so that we would be able to follow them. I was confident that Shardas and Luka would find me, and then we would get Velika back.

I had to believe it.

A quick tour of the islet revealed nothing growing and nothing edible, but I did find a few sticks and one smallish driftwood log that had washed ashore. I piled them up, pulled the flint and tinder from my belt pouch, and lit them. My signal fire was so pitiful that I soon added the scraps of fabric left over from my gown that were too small to be of use, some loose twigs from the basket, and then my own undertunic.

If I needed to, I would burn the linen wrappings for the gown, and then the basket.

If I needed to, I would burn the gown itself.

When Shardas came roaring and splashing down into the water beside my islet, the last of the linen had burned, and I was reaching for the basket.

"Creel!" Luka threw himself off Shardas and into the water, thrashed up onto the islet, and embraced me. I greeted him with equal enthusiasm: in fact, to my embarrassment, I began to cry.

"Th-they t-t-took her, I don't know where," I sobbed into his shoulder, while Shardas roared and sent spurts of water in every direction. Overhead other dragons circled, dragons I knew, like Niva and Feniul, who would have died rather than betray their queen.

"Both of you calm down!" Luka had to shout to be heard.

"Where is she?" Shardas's eyes glowed with rage.

I sniffled. "I'm sorry. I didn't realize they had other dragons to help them—"

Shardas's gaze softened and he swallowed the flames coming from his mouth.

"Creel, I am not blaming you," he said in a gentler voice. "We all . . . Pots of firebane were thrown out of the jungle at us, and we were all helpless," he explained. "I would never expect you to defend Velika alone. Did you see which direction they went?"

Gulping, I pointed to the arrows I had drawn in the sand. Part of my drawing had been washed away by Shardas's violent arrival, and with a squawk I ran to retrace the lines before they disappeared entirely.

"I didn't think there was anything in that direction," Shardas said, studying the arrows and looking out across the water. "South and east? You are certain?"

"Yes."

"Then that's where we're going." He lifted his head and roared out something in the dragon language. It was loud and harsh, and Luka and I put our hands over our ears until it was over. Then he turned to us. "Get on."

Luka grabbed my basket and Shardas obligingly held out a foreleg. We managed to get on his back without dunking, and Shardas took off as soon as we were settled.

"Where's Hagen? Is he all right?" I had to turn my head around as far as I could and shout the question, we were going so fast.

"He's coming with supplies," said Luka. "I think that's what the dragontalk was about. Shardas has the rest of them waiting back on the islands. As soon as we find anything, they are going to gather food and follow."

"How long since they left you?" Shardas called back to me, his speed never wavering.

"Since dawn."

It seemed impossible, but he put on more speed, and Luka and I could do nothing but hunker down and cling like burrs. The usual exhilaration of flying was gone, stolen away by fear, and anger, and wind.

Frock Coat and Pigs' Teeth

We flew for days on end, and would have given in to despair except for little signs our quarry left behind, giving us hope. There was no real land, but here and there tiny clusters of islets would provide rest and clues. We found signs of fresh fires, dragon claw marks, and recently shed scales of dull brown and green, proving we were on the right path.

"I never knew the ocean was so vast," I said helplessly one morning as I climbed up on Shardas's shoulders with Luka.

"I don't think anyone did," Luka replied, grim.

We were all feeling bleak. Shardas's raging had subsided into a dreadful silence, broken only by the occasional grunted answer to a direct question.

Hagen and a horde of other dragons caught up with us at one of the islets. I invited my brother to trade places with Luka so that we might ride together for a while, but Hagen told me that he much preferred riding on Feniul, who looked less likely to suddenly turn violent.

While I agreed that Shardas looked near his breaking point, it was all the more reason for me not to abandon him.

So whenever he held out his foreleg, I clambered up and took my customary seat, with Luka behind me.

And we flew.

We came at last to a long, low island, curved like a sickle and covered with tall palm trees. We landed on the shore to rest, and a host of men in rough, brown kilts came out of the trees, wielding spears and shouting.

Luka leaped off Shardas's back and went toward them with hands outstretched. I signaled to Hagen to stay on Feniul and went to stand beside Luka. I'm sure we looked a sight: sunburned and filthy, Luka's hair standing on end and mine unraveling from its double-dozen braids.

And then there was the fleet of dragons with us.

Using hand gestures, Luka tried to signal to them that we wanted only to rest here, but the leader of the men was adamant that we go. He seemed particularly agitated by the dragons. Not frightened by them, I noticed, just insistent that they leave. He indicated that we humans could stay, but that our friends were not welcome.

"So they have seen dragons, and they don't like them," Luka said in an undertone.

I looked at our friends. They were all tired. Their scales were crusted with salt and several of them were twitching the nets strung over their backs, wanting to scoop up some fish and eat. Shardas looked like he was losing his patience, lashing his tail and snorting hot little bursts of air.

Then a man came out of the trees wearing an incongruous red frock coat over his kilt and bearing a staff decorated with pigs' teeth. I identified his coat as of Roulaini make, and whispered as much to Luka.

The man bowed his head gracefully, and asked a question in what I recognized as Citatian, even though my grasp of that language had never been good. With obvious relief, Luka replied in the same language, and they talked for some minutes, the man occasionally gesturing with his staff.

When both Luka and the man were satisfied, they nodded cordially and the spear-carrying men retreated. All but two, that is, and their leader in his frock coat. They stood on the sand and watched us as we walked back to Shardas and the others.

"That was very unexpected," Luka said.

"He's been to the Grand Market at Pelletie," I guessed.

"His family goes every ten years or so," Luka confirmed. "He says that we can rest here, and fish," he went on in a louder voice, and most of the dragons dispersed to gather food or sprawl on the sand.

Niva and her mate, Leontes, Amacarin, Feniul, and Shardas remained to hear what else Luka had to say. Hagen slid down off Feniul and came to my side, putting an arm around my shoulders so heavily that it nearly dragged me to my knees. We were all so tired I didn't know if we would even be able to fight Darrym and the others when we caught up to them.

"They flew overhead only last night," Luka said. "They didn't land, though. They know that they aren't welcome here."

"So these people have had dealings with Darrym's dragons, and the people with them, before?" Leontes, an alchemist, was peering keenly at our three watchers as he asked.

"Some. Not long ago the dragons came here, towing people in those baskets, and asked questions by drawing figures in the sand. They wanted to know if there were any dragons living here, if dragons had ever been seen here, and what colors the dragons were."

"Strange," Leontes said slowly.

"The only ones who had ever seen a dragon before were the chief's family, who had been to Citatie and seen dragons there, so the visitors flew on. A week later a half dozen dragons arrived and tried to capture the people of this island, but they managed to fight the attackers off."

"Stranger and stranger," Leontes commented.

"You can see why they don't want a whole army of dragons landing on the beach," Hagen said.

"Precisely," Luka said. "I had to assure him over and over that we weren't going to attack, that we were just passing through. I think the news that we had been attacked by one of those hostile dragons, and were looking to fight with them, was what really persuaded them to let us rest here."

"Will they help us?" I looked over at the three men watching us, but their faces were expressionless. "Would they send any warriors with us, to fight Darrym's people?"

"I'll ask, but I don't think so," Luka said.

While we were eating, Luka did ask Frock Coat if he would send some men with us but the response was a resounding "No!" Apparently they had their hands full dealing with an island nation to the west that occasionally sent an invading force against them.

"Do they know how far it is to wherever Darrym is headed?" I fastened my sewing basket to Shardas's spine ridges and then sat down in front of it.

"No," Luka said. "They've never gone that far. But they also believe that there is a land even farther to the southeast that is the home of the gods, and they don't want to risk the gods' wrath by trespassing. The farthest anyone from here has gone is two days' journey by boat, and there was no sign of land."

"Two days' journey by boat is a matter of hours to me," Shardas said, speaking for the first time since we'd landed. "And Darrym is not a god." He flung himself into the air.

Dark Forests

"How is it that no one in Feravel has ever heard of a country this large?"

We had landed on a small mountain that jutted from the water just off the shore of a country that was dark with forest. Country? No, it was a continent, stretching in all directions as far as we could see. Great mist-wreathed mountains rose in the distance, covered with exotic trees: dark green and twisted in shape, with odd spiky leaves.

"I don't know," Luka said in a hushed voice. "But without a dragon it would have taken months to get here."

"Winter storms would likely have sunk the ships if anyone had tried," Leontes said. "And if they couldn't find fresh water . . ." He surveyed the landscape. "And then there are superstitions that keep some people from exploring."

"Like that the home of the gods lies in this direction?" Luka snorted. "I'll wager Darrym and his friends started that rumor themselves, so that no one would bother them."

"But why? What are they doing?" I pounded my fist on Shardas's shoulder in frustration.

We had found this country, had even found a wide clearing in the trees near the shoreline that was the start of a dragon-sized path and marked with recent signs that Darrym and the others had passed that way. Taking refuge on this mountain a little ways offshore, we hoped to spy on Velika's captors, but they had disappeared into the forest.

We were at a loss as to what to do next.

"We need to go down into the forest and look for them," I said.

"But how?" Luka held out his arms. "You saw what the people looked like, Creel. We'll never pass as being from around here, and neither will the dragons."

"Not without disguises," Leontes said.

"I'm not putting a spike through my nose," Hagen piped up. "I'm sorry . . . I'll do whatever else." He gave a little shudder. "But no spikes through my nose. And how did they make those white tattoos?"

Leontes gave a huff of laughter. "I meant the dragons, actually. We can all speak in dragon tongue, but you cannot speak the language of these humans."

"But how can we dye your scales?" I looked him over. He was a buttery yellow color with violet streaks, and nearly twice the size of Darrym. "And all the dragons with Darrym are small."

"A physical disguise won't work," Leontes agreed. "But an alchemical one might."

I held my breath and looked at Shardas. Though he had lived with a human alchemist for many years following Velika's supposed death, he objected to dragons using alchemy. I had thought this was due to Velika's betrayal by King Milun the First, but then I learned that Shardas's brother, Krashath, had also used alchemy to enslave their own people. Now I waited for Shardas to object to Leontes's plan.

But Shardas never took his eyes off the path into the forest. "What supplies will you need?" he asked Leontes.

As it turned out, Leontes was prepared for any contingency. Strapped to his back was a large, leather-bound trunk which he had filled with various potions, powders, and tools that were the staples of an alchemist's practice. The only extra ingredients he needed to transform a half dozen of our large, brightly hued friends into the small, dull, forest-blending enemy dragons were scales.

"There are plenty of those," Feniul said, and raised one foreclaw to his neck. "How many do you require?"

"I'm afraid that I need scales from these brown and green dragons," Leontes clarified. "In order to get the look right. We'll have to sneak down off the mountain and get a few."

"How many?" Luka and I asked at the same time.

"At least three, and from different dragons," Leontes said. "So that our spies don't all look precisely the same."

"All right," I said. "We'll wait until dark, and then someone can fly us down to the shore. Luka and I can scrounge up some scales and you can make the potion."

"It's a paste," Leontes corrected me. "Niva is the darkest, and might appear the closest in color to the dragons we've seen, if she stays in the shadow of the trees. Feniul's green scales are rather . . . bright."

"I want to come, too," Hagen said.

"No." I folded my arms. "Absolutely not."

"If you're going, I'm going," he insisted.

"I'm used to this type of danger," I began.

"I'm older than you were when you fought in the First Dragon War," Hagen interrupted.

Leontes's eyes twinkled as he broke in, stopping me from replying. "I could use some assistance in preparing the paste," he told Hagen. "A pair of human hands would be welcome."

Hagen hesitated, torn between his desire to be included in what he no doubt saw as an adventure and helping an honest-to-Caxon alchemist prepare one of his secret recipes. "All right," he said finally.

"There are some hours still until dark," Shardas said. "And my scales are even brighter than Feniul's." He heaved a sigh. "We should find a place to make camp where we can all be concealed."

In the end we located a small island a few leagues offshore, just large enough for our army to encamp. It was craggy enough that the dragons could hide in the crevices during the brightest parts of the day, and far enough from the mainland that Velika's captors would have a hard time seeing us anyway.

Still, Shardas ordered everyone to avoid flying or flaming unless completely necessary, and for as many as possible of us to stay on the seaward side of the island. It was not a luxurious spot, but it would have to do.

"I'm not expecting to be here long," Shardas said as I settled on a rock to work on my wedding gown until nightfall.

Luka had obligingly gone to fish with Amacarin so that he wouldn't see it. "We'll find Velika in the next day or so, get her out, and go home."

My only answer was a nod. Seeing this vast country, so thickly covered by forests and mountains, I didn't know how we could possibly succeed. Velika could be anywhere, and she was so near to laying her eggs that I had a constant knot in my stomach over that alone.

A sudden roaring distracted me from my grim thoughts, and I stuffed my gown into the basket and jumped to my feet. The dragons were all supposed to stay quiet, but I could discern more than one voice crying out. Shardas was just rising into the air to go toward the sound—which seemed to come from the other side of the island—when the water in front of us fountained upward.

I shielded my face against the spray, and when I could look I saw Niva floating in the water, looking triumphant. She had the draglines of a fishing net in her foreclaws, and tangled within the net was a small, gray dragon with only one pair of horns, like a cow.

A rebel.

"It seems that Luka and Creel will not need to go foraging for scales tonight after all," she said, preening. "True, we will look somewhat the same, but . . ."

"But it is a small price to pay," Shardas agreed, his eyes gleaming, "to avoid endangering ourselves. And, we will be able to question this dragon as an added bonus."

Confused, the little, gray dragon's head swung from side to

side, watching Niva and Shardas. It was plain that he couldn't understand Feravelan. Shardas cleared his throat and asked the captive something in the dragon tongue, which I understood even with my limited knowledge of the language.

"Where is the queen?"

Fade to Gray

Shardas's question hung in the air, and the young dragon moaned and stopped struggling. His eyes rolled and he looked shocked and horrified. I wondered if the colors of my friends seemed grotesque to him, much as Feniul and the others pitied Darrym and his dull scales.

Giving him a little shake, Niva repeated her king's question, and at last the little dragon began to talk.

And talk.

I could hardly blame him: he was young, he was trapped in a net, and he was surrounded by very large, very foreign, and very angry dragons. When he stumbled over his words or stopped for a breath, Shardas prodded him with more questions and on he went again. I heartily wished I had taken the time to learn more than the two dozen or so words Shardas had taught me. Feniul tried to translate, but it was too difficult for him to keep up with Shardas's furious questions, so after a while he stopped and gave Luka, Hagen, and me the gist of it later.

By a stroke of the most blessed luck, this little dragon was in fact Darrym's brother, though he had never met Darrym until yesterday. It seemed that this was indeed Darrym's homeland, and he and other young male dragons had been sent out years ago to search for the queen dragon and bring her back, because their people needed her. Why, the little dragon wouldn't tell at first, except to say there would be more hatchlings now, and they would be bigger and stronger.

Even though Darrym had spent years in the collar of the Citatian army, he was returning home a hero. He had found Velika, signaled his fellow searchers, and brought the queen to his people. She was now being held in something called a "lesser temple." They were especially excited that she would soon have hatchlings of her own, which raised the hackles on my neck.

I did not want Velika to have to lay her eggs in captivity, and I certainly didn't want them hatching here. I could see by Shardas's eyes that he felt the same, and Niva looked as though she might be sick.

"What right have you to steal the queen?" Feniul was outraged. "What right have you to lock her away? She is your queen, too!"

"But that's why we need her." Feniul translated the little dragon's whine. "We're the chosen people, and we're dying off! No eggs have hatched in two years! We need the queen and you don't! She's brought you enough blessings. Now it's our turn!" He gestured at the dragons gathered around: huge and glowing with their jewel-like colors.

"What shall I do with him?" Niva gave the little dragon a shake so that he would stop sniveling.

"Get however many scales Leontes requires," Shardas instructed. "Then find a way to keep him penned up. We can't have him carrying news of us back to Darrym. Or anyone else, for that matter."

"Is that enough? Won't they come searching for him?" Hagen's brows were nearly touching over his nose.

I gave him an alarmed look. "We are not going to kill this dragon, Hagen."

"Of course not!" Now *he* looked alarmed, and rather shocked. "I was just thinking that maybe we could take some of its hoard, and hold that hostage in exchange for him keeping quiet."

"Oh." I was a little embarrassed that I had presumed my brother was suggesting something so horrible, and then impressed at the very clever suggestion he *was* making.

Shardas thought about it and then asked the dragon what it hoarded, in a seemingly casual way (as far as I could tell). He had to ask twice to make himself understood, though, and then the hostage's answer seemed to take him aback.

Turning to us, Shardas said, "He collects people."

"I beg your pardon?" My eyebrows shot toward my hairline.

"He collects people," Shardas repeated.

"And you thought I was odd for collecting dogs!" Amusement warred with horror on Feniul's face.

"That's not quite right. . . ." Shardas shook his head. "He doesn't seem to understand what a hoard is, but says he doesn't yet have his own . . . people. Odd."

"Very," I agreed, puzzled.

Luka shook his head in confusion. "Are you sure the information he's giving us is correct?" He frowned at the little dragon. "Hey . . . you?" He glanced at Shardas. "What's his name, at least?"

Shardas asked, and then looked surprised again.

"His name's probably something like Little Peder No-People," Luka said.

"Gray Whiner," Hagen suggested, and I used both elbows to poke their ribs.

"He doesn't have a name," Shardas said, "because he's not old enough and he doesn't have a . . . hoard of people . . . yet."

"How old do you have to be to have a name and a hoard?" Hagen wanted to know.

"Twenty," Shardas translated.

"He won't have a name until he's twenty? That's awful," Hagen said.

Shardas's eyes were hard. "These dragons have fallen far from our traditions," he said, and the other dragons nodded in agreement. "Secure him somewhere out of the way, Niva. Leontes, take the scales you need and get to work."

Leontes did get to work, with Hagen to assist him, and Luka and I went with Niva to secure the little gray dragon. Luka insisted on calling him Peder No-People, but since he couldn't understand us, the gray dragon wasn't offended.

I kept peppering our captive with questions through Niva. I was fascinated by these strange, dull-colored dragons and the people that they apparently collected.

When I had seen the humans with Darrym, I had assumed that Darrym was acting under their direction. But now I realized it must be the other way around.

It was indeed the dragons who were in charge.

This made me uneasy, not because I balked at the idea of dragons running a country, but because if these dragons were willing to take their own queen captive, the Triunity alone knew what other harm they were capable of. I said this aloud, and Luka shook his head.

"Not as much harm as Shardas, if we don't find Velika soon," he pointed out, and I agreed.

"I do feel sorry for them," I said, indicating the little dragon, which looked very forlorn with the net fouling his wings and pinning him to the ground. "They need Shardas and Velika to help them, if it's true that they're all small and sickly, but this was the wrong way to go about getting that help."

"What could Shardas and Velika have done?" Luka came to put his arm around me, and I leaned into his side.

"Helped them find other, stronger dragons to mate with, so they didn't die out," I suggested. "Made them stop collecting people."

"Would that really help them?" He looked skeptical.

"Collecting humans is wrong," Niva said stridently. "And whether or not it would help them have healthier hatchlings, it must be stopped."

"Well, I'm not arguing with that," Luka said.

Suddenly, there was an explosion from behind the rock where Hagen was helping Leontes with his alchemy, and we hurried to make sure they were all right. Peder No-People gave a piteous little moan as we three turned our backs on him, but this only made Niva check his bonds, and then we left him there anyway.

But both Leontes and Hagen were unharmed and looking mightily pleased with themselves when we climbed over the boulders. In a large copper cauldron was a thick, gray paste with red and brown flecks in it. There was a faint gray haze in the air: the last trace of the explosion, which smelled of salt.

Waving the cloud away, Leontes looked beyond us to Shardas, who had also come to see what had happened. "It is finished, my king," he said. "Sooner than I expected, but according to the description in the scrolls, it looks precisely as it should. Although there is only enough for three."

Shardas eyed the paste, sniffing delicately. "Does one . . . eat that?" He was willing to overcome his aversion to alchemy for Velika's sake, but within reason.

"No, no!" Leontes assured us. "It is to be smeared over your scales." He looked at the position of the sun. "And we had best start now, if you want us to be completely covered by dark. Who is it to be?"

"Amacarin," Shardas answered promptly. "He is larger than these dragons, but not by much. And myself, despite my size." Then he hesitated, and I knew precisely why.

The only other dragon small enough to aid the illusion was Feniul. Feniul, who was not particularly known for his spying abilities and who dithered over the least little decision. Niva would be the better choice, but given her size, the illusion would not work as well on her. It would be hard enough to conceal Shardas's extra bulk.

"Let me go, cousin," Feniul said quietly, coming into the rock hollow, which was rapidly becoming crowded. "I can do this, for Velika."

Shardas studied the smaller dragon, and then nodded. "Feniul, Amacarin, and I," he said.

"And I'm going with you," I announced.

"Creel—," Luka began.

I cut him off with a look. "You can come with me, but if you try to prevent me from going I will have Niva tie you up with Peder No-People," I said, my voice brooking no argument.

"Hagen," Leontes said, "you will need to rub this paste on Shardas and the others. And I will make a stain for Luka and Creel's hair and skin, which you may find interesting."

This alarmed me more than the prospect of going into the forest in search of hostile dragons and their pet humans. "A *stain*? Will it come off?" I imagined myself at my wedding in my beautiful white gown, with weird muddy streaks on my skin and in my hair.

"If it doesn't wash out naturally by the end of the week, I can concoct something that will strip it out overnight," Leontes said with great assurance.

"You had blue hair for six months," Luka said.

"There's a difference," I said stiffly. "I was trying to start a new fashion." Actually, I had been trying to blend in with the Citatians by using a dye that I had been told would wash out in a matter of weeks. Instead it had taken months, by the end of which the color was faded and the dyed strands had become dull and stringy.

"Blue hair?" Hagen hooted with laughter. "Thank the Triunity that didn't catch on! Blue!"

"Here's the paste," I said, and I shoved a large wooden spoon into his hands.

I took another spoon and began spreading the concoction on Shardas's shoulder. The paste began to dissolve as soon as I smeared it on, leaving behind scales that had faded from gold to gray.

"Will it work?" Shardas twisted his neck to peer at his shoulder.

"It has to," I whispered.

Into the Forest

Peder No-People had said that Velika was being held in a lesser temple. He clearly did not know which one, and when asked how you found any of these lesser temples, he only looked confused. There were no roads, it seemed; you simply walked in the right direction until you found one, Peder insisted.

And the right direction, according to the nameless little, gray dragon, was *in*.

"In the mountains, do you suppose?" Luka leaned forward to whisper into my ear as we tentatively moved into the first stand of trees on the mainland. Shardas, Feniul, and Amacarin were flanking us. "In a cave?"

"He claims the caves are poisonous," Shardas said.

"How can a cave be poisonous?" I rolled my eyes, assuming it was something the little dragon had been told to keep him out from underfoot.

"Easily, if there are fissures in the earth, with fumes and gases leaking out of them," Luka said. "My sense is that these mountains are former volcanoes like those on the Far Isles and in the Boiling Sea, only newer. It's possible some are even still active and leaking gases. It would explain why these dragons are dying, as well."

I shuddered and he didn't need to explain any further. The Boiling Sea, on the edge of the King's Seat, was a vast churning horror of noxious gases and water hot enough to kill a human on contact. I had no urge to investigate the caves here, if they were anything like a land version of the Boiling Sea.

Silent now, we crept through the forest.

Since I had no idea how to emulate the white tattoos or convoluted clothing of Velika's captors, or if their women even wore such things. I was wearing Citatian trousers and a tunic that Leontes had helped me dye a dull brown. At the very least I would blend into the trees. Luka, too, had blushingly declined the bandage-like wrappings Leontes offered and wore a pair of trousers cut off at the knee and a leather vest.

Looking at Shardas and the others really did give one a turn, though. They appeared small and dull, yet if you looked closer you could see the tree branches being pushed aside by the true reach of Shardas's head, or his furled wings. My friends appeared shrunken, and yet they were not.

In this manner we continued into the forest, tripping over roots and rocks, with only the filtered light of the moons to assure us we were headed at all in the right direction. Of course, "in" was such a vague bearing that it wasn't hard to follow. We saw neither scale nor claw of another dragon, and no humans seemed to be in evidence, either, which made us relax more than we should have.

When my bootlace came undone, I told the others to go

ahead. It turned out to be broken, and it took me longer than I had thought to knot it and refasten the boot. So when I finally stood up, and found myself face-to-face with a woman with her hair piled high on her head and white triangles marching across her cheeks, I'm not sure who was more surprised.

Before I could even yell she grabbed my arm and hustled me off to the right, hissing and snarling at me in a strange tongue and gesticulating with her free hand. I opened my mouth to shout the alarm, but she slapped her hand across my face to stop me. I writhed, trying to break free, but her hands were like steel clamped across my bicep and face, and I could only thrash and whimper ineffectually as she dragged me over a fallen tree trunk and into a small clearing where three other women squatted around a small fire with a bubbling cauldron hanging over it.

They all looked quite startled to see me, and I could hardly blame them. These were the first women from this country that I had seen, and I knew at a glance that I would never pass for one of them.

They were dressed even more elaborately than the men, and their many-layered skirts, if they could be called such, barely reached to mid-thigh. The bodices were little more than a strip of cloth, but it was wound around the bust several times and knotted in a decorative fashion. Both pieces of clothing were made of coarse, brown cloth, striped with dull red or darker brown. Necklaces, too many to count, hung in tangles from throat to waist, and were festooned with feathers and seashells as well as beads of bone, gold, and wood. Both nostrils had been pierced, as well as their ears, and each woman had at least half a dozen earrings per lobe. Their hair, shiny black and straight, was tied up high on their heads and charms and baubles dangled from it. Everywhere skin showed—cheeks, arms, legs—white symbols had been imprinted on it.

And there I stood, with my hair in a double-dozen braids and wearing a badly dyed Citatian tunic and trousers.

We stared at one another for a long time, and then the woman who had seized me said something and used the hand she had over my mouth to twist my head around to face her. In the moonlight and firelight, she stared at my eyes with an expression of disgusted fascination. Then her companions came and joined her. The youngest of them, who seemed to be approximately my age, made as if to poke my eye.

"Hey!" I jerked away as best I could: my captor still had a viselike grip on my jaw.

It was then that it occurred to me that perhaps they had never seen blue eyes before, and dyeing my hair and skin had been a pointless ruse when my foreignness was plain to see whenever I blinked. This realization made me sag in the woman's fierce grip, and she let me sink down on one of the logs they were using for seats.

Their rapid discussion went on around me, while I silently shouted for Luka and Shardas. I was so caught up in this that it took me a moment to realize they had directed their conversation at me. The woman who had grabbed me spoke at length, waving her arms about, but I could only shrug no matter how she yelled.

Seeing that she was not going to give up until I gave her a

better answer than a shrug, I decided to pantomime. I made my fingers walk down my arm, and then stopped, tapped one cheek and looked around with a confused expression, as though lost. Then I smiled and shrugged at her. I was only an innocent girl, lost in a big forest.

Who just happened to be dressed funny and have strangely colored eyes.

She didn't believe me, and I didn't blame her.

While she stood guard over me, the other three women—all of them younger and, I suspected, daughters or nieces, for there was a strong resemblance beneath the markings on their faces—collected their things. They carefully decanted the bubbling mixture from the cauldron into stoneware jars, which they sealed with red wax and some chanting. There were herbs laid out in rows on a cloth; these were gently tied with string, rolled up, and stowed in leather packs. When all this was done, and dirt poured on the fire to put it out, we began to walk. We headed "in," but at an angle away from the direction my friends and I had been traveling and I felt my stomach twist with anxiety. How would Luka and the others find me? And if I got free on my own, could I find them?

The woman pushed me ahead of her, hissing in annoyance when I stumbled, guiding me farther into the forest and the darkness. We walked for hours, until I thought my toes were broken from kicking unseen rocks, and I wanted to scream with the tension of not knowing where I was going and how I would get back to where I belonged.

The trees parted ahead of us just as dawn was breaking

greenly through the leaves. Before me was a village of wooden huts, peopled by white-marked men and women and children, all sporting strings of beads and feathers, and all eager to come and stare at the strange blue-eyed girl thrown into their midst.

Village Life

The woman who had captured me was a person of great importance, I came to understand. I was taken to the largest hut, which was hers, and all of the villagers save for her three daughters stopped short in the yard as though an invisible barrier prevented them from coming any closer. Looking around the village, I could see people running in and out of one another's dwellings, spreading the gossip about me, but this hut they did not enter.

The hut had no coverings on the windows or doors, however, so I was still perfectly visible to the group assembled outside as I was pushed down onto a woven grass floor mat. A finger was shaken in my face and I was ordered not to move, or so I gathered. Then the women went about the hut, putting away the herbs and carefully storing the jars of fresh-brewed potions, ignoring me and their gawking, whispering neighbors.

After everything had been put away, the younger women sat down to eat something that looked terrible but smelled wonderful. Their mother—I had decided that she must be their mother—went to the doorway and pointed imperiously at a young boy in the crowd. He came forward, bare chest puffed out with importance, received some instructions from my captor, and took off at a run.

Then at last she turned to me. Looking me up and down and speaking as though to an idiot, she asked me something. I shrugged and shook my head.

Gesturing at her chest, she let loose with a string of syllables that went on for a full breath. Then she turned and said something about each of her daughters that sounded just as complex. She pointed to me again, and raised her eyebrows.

Gathering that she had just told me their names, and asked me mine, I hesitated, but reckoned there was no reason to conceal my identity. They wouldn't know me from the next foreigner. "Creel," I said.

She looked startled, and one of her daughters burst out laughing. My cheeks burned: did my name have some wildly inappropriate meaning in their tongue?

But with a look of unbearable smugness the youngest girl repeated her own name, and then said, "Creel," before bursting into peals of laughter.

Perhaps not inappropriate, but apparently embarrassingly short, and I didn't think that trying to explain my full name, Creelisel Carlbrun, would do much to repair the damage. So I just stared at the youngest daughter until she became self-conscious and stopped.

The mother, whose name started out as something that sounded like Ullalal, offered me some of the strange food on a wooden plate. I ate a little, using my fingers to scoop it up the way they did. It had a rich flavor that I liked very much, until a slow burn started on my tongue and continued down my throat. My eyes and nose began to stream, and I had to put down the plate hastily.

This caused much laughter among all three daughters, but finally one of them poured me a cup of what turned out to be sour milk. It helped with the burning, but the taste made me gag. I thought perhaps she was taunting me further, but when my eyes cleared I saw them all pouring themselves cups from the same pitcher.

By gulping the sour milk in between bites of the spicy food, I was able to bolt it all down, where I sincerely hoped that it would stay. I would need to keep my strength up if I wanted to escape.

The other villagers were still outside the hut staring in, but as my captor and her daughters set out mats and lay down to rest, the gawkers began to drift away. It seemed odd that they would sleep so early in the day—it was not yet noon—but I supposed that they were tired out from their nocturnal herb-gathering expedition. Even more odd was that, before they lay down, they covered their white tattoos with small leather patches the exact size and shape of the markings. As they positioned the mats in the full glare of the sunlight, it dawned on me: they weren't white tattoos, they were untanned patches of skin! This truly was an alien land. . . .

I had been tied by the ankle to the thick support pole in the center of the hut and given a mat to lie on as well, but couldn't sleep. I lay still, listening to their restful breathing, and wondering how I would get out of here and find Luka and the others.

And if they were looking for me.

And if they had found Velika.

Once my captors were asleep, I silently tested my bonds. A leather cord had been used to tether me, and the knot was so tight that it would have to be cut; there was simply no way to undo it. I gave it my best try, though, and only succeeded in breaking off a nail so close to the quick that it stung and bled. I lay back, sucking my finger and pondering whether they would cut my bonds so that I could relieve myself (an idea that was becoming more pressing than hypothetical), and if I would be able to make a run for it then.

I had a fairly good sense of direction, and thought that we were west of where I had been separated from my friends. If I went in that direction, I would eventually come out on the shore within sight of the islet where we were encamped, and it would be easy to signal to them. It was a thin hope, but it was all I had.

I had just started rubbing my bonds against a rough piece of floorboard when the midmorning nap was interrupted by a loud clanging. Instantly everyone in the hut but me was on their feet. Mats were rolled up and pushed aside, including my own, from which one of the daughters rousted me with an angry slap on the leg. They cut the leather thong that tied me, but only to loop another one around my wrists and use it to drag me from the hut. It bit into my flesh and I stumbled, trying to keep up so that they wouldn't tug on it so hard.

The entire population was gathered in the center of the village, where there was a crude bell hanging from a pole. The boy who had been sent running by my chief captor was there, practically swinging from the leather strap that dangled down. The villagers cleared a path so that I could be taken right up to the bell, which the boy finally stopped ringing. Everyone turned to face a circle of beaten earth surrounded by stones half-buried in the ground. They knelt, and I was forced down with them.

There was a flap and rush, and a dragon soared down to land inside the ring. I lifted my head, and someone reached out and pushed it down again. Looking up from beneath my eyelashes, I could see that this wasn't a dragon I knew. It was almost as large as Feniul, and gray with black splotches on its back and flanks. It surveyed the kneeling villagers with a satisfied expression, then turned to me and the women surrounding me.

With a sickening plummet of my stomach, I realized that this village belonged to the gray dragon, and I was about to be added to its collection.

Ullalal and the dragon discussed me at some length, while I fidgeted and looked for the quickest route through the gathered villagers and into the forest. I was so busy looking for a way to sneak off that it took me several seconds to realize that they had stopped talking and were now just looking at me. The dragon made an imperious gesture with one foreclaw, beckoning me closer, and Ullalal grabbed my arm.

I refused to crawl, which she tried to get me to do by pushing at my legs with one hand and holding my back down with the other. I shook her off and stood, walking forward to stand just outside the ring of stones. I was feeling bold, but not insane. I bowed to the dragon and laid a hand on my chest.

"My name is Creel."

The dragon studied me, scratching at its neck idly. It was just finishing molting some old scales, and a few still clung to its neck and along its back, where it was hard to reach.

Last year I had helped Shardas peel away the scales that had been burned in his dive into the Boiling Sea to rescue Velika, and I was an expert at it. They smarted unless you wiggled them as you pulled, and you had to make sure that they were really ready to come loose before you even did that. It was not unlike easing out a loose baby tooth for humans.

"Allow me," I said, and reached out to a loose scale. I gave a light tug, felt it loosen, and wiggled it free.

The village was so silent that a door curtain flapping on a hut nearby sounded loud and sinister. From the horrified silence all around me, I was guessing that I had just done something very, very taboo. I looked at the scale in my hand, not certain now what to do with it, and wondered numbly if I was about to be burned to ash.

I had only been trying to befriend the dragon, to ingratiate myself, really. It had occurred to me that if I showed that I meant no harm, was eager to be of use, in fact, maybe I could convince it to take me where there were more dragons. And one of those dragons might lead me to Velika.

The silence stretched. Then the dragon sniffed me, his huffing breath breaking the quiet. He asked me something, and I shook my head, uncomprehending. He switched to the dragon tongue, and asked me who I belonged to. I understood this, roughly, but refused to claim I belonged to anyone. Besides which: speaking dragon would ruin a human throat.

As I had with Ullalal the night before, I just smiled and shook my head.

With reverent hands, Ullalal took the scale from me and placed it in a pouch at her waist. I realized suddenly that she was an alchemist. It would explain her prominence in the village, her strange collection of herbs, and also the others' fear of her hut.

"I need *klgaosh*," the dragon, whose name was Rannym, said.

I didn't know what that last word was, but Ullalal looked rather annoyed, an expression she quickly covered. I heard a small gasp from the kneeling crowd, and turned my head a little to look. Ullalal's youngest daughter had dared to raise her head, and she was looking at me with an expression of jealousy and almost palpable hatred. I rocked back at the force of her glare. Perhaps she had hoped to be the new *klgaosh*. I suppressed a desire to look smug.

"I carry you," the dragon said next.

Stepping around him, I put out a hand to his side. He being smaller than Amacarin, I would hardly need help in climbing up. But another shocked silence settled upon the village, and the dragon gave a snort of outrage. A foreclaw shot out and fastened around my waist uncomfortably tight. He leaped into the air with me hanging breathless from one claw, while below us the villagers raised their voices in a strange, ululating cry. I pushed my fears aside and concentrated on trying to breathe despite the claw clamped around my middle.

The New Klgaosh

J ust when I thought I might throw up from the pressure on
my stomach, the dragon descended into the forest. It had
been quite disconcerting to dangle above the trees in that way,
and I had worried—along with my concern about breathing—
that he might lose his grip and drop me onto some spiky
branches. But at last he set me down in a small clearing, just in
front of a large wooden shed. It was festooned with garlands of
shells and beads, and wreaths of evergreen branches that now
belied their name by being brown and dry.

This was the dragon's home, and if a *klgaosh* was a personal servant, as I suspected, than the last one had been
gone for some time. Mud had been tracked into the shed, several of the garlands were dangling down into the dirt, and
there was a spiderweb curtaining part of the doorway. The
only sign of recent habitation was the carcass of a deer near
the doorway, which had been well picked over by the dragon,
but not enough to discourage swarms of flies. I wrinkled my
nose and wondered if I might be sick after all.

The dragon nudged me toward the carcass. I gave him a
blank look. What in the name of the Triunity was I supposed
to do with a deer carcass as big as I was?

Heaving a mighty sigh, the dragon led me over to a large pit at the back of the shed. Pungent lime had been sprinkled over the contents, which appeared to be more remains from his dinners. It burned my eyes, but at least the lime kept the flies away and made the meat decompose more quickly. It was just one more shocking difference to discover that these drag-ons didn't cook their meat first.

Gritting my teeth while the dragon looked on impatiently, I grabbed the hind hooves of the deer and dragged it around the shed to the pit. I couldn't really throw it in, and had to settle for pulling it to the edge and letting it roll down the slope. Then I grabbed a scoop of lime from the nearby barrel, one sleeve held over my nose and mouth, and sprinkled it lib-erally over the carcass.

This satisfied the dragon, and he took me back to the front of his home, gestured around with a claw, and ordered me to clean it. Then he bunched his hind legs and sprang into the air, leaving me standing near the spiderweb, alone, sweaty, and frustrated.

With nothing better to do, I searched his house. I found a pallet at the back, and a few strings of beads and strips of cloth that had probably been my predecessor's feast-day best. There was a cupboard that contained pots of uncooked rice and other food items, some of which had gone bad, and a broom and various cleaning tools. In the middle of the house was a huge pile of branches, leaves, and grasses that was the dragon's bed. They were all dry and brittle, and mice scut-tled out of my way when I kicked at it experimentally.

"Well, this is just disgusting," I said to the mice.

There was a rake in the cupboard, and I took it out and attacked the dragon's bed, hauling great rake-fulls of dried material outside. I made a pile to one side and determined to have the dragon burn it when he returned. The mice ran out, terrified, and I shook my fist at them as they left. They might look sweet, as Marta claimed, but I knew that they were disease-ridden little creatures that did not belong anywhere near a human habitation. I used the broom to sweep the floor, and knocked down the spiderweb and the spider in it.

I shook some ants out of the bucket, and wandered through the trees until I found a quick-running stream. I carried bucket after bucket into the barnlike dwelling and sluiced the floor clean, since there was nothing resembling a mop. I took the human-sized pallet outside and beat it until the sweetgrass stuffing threatened to burst out, then left it in the sun to air.

My arms ached, my lower back ached, and my eyes were stinging with dust. The forest was so thick that very little sunlight filtered down, and now that my sweat was drying I was cold.

Since my new master still had not returned, I decided to have a look around without the forest getting in my way. I selected a tree with sturdy, ladderlike branches and began to climb. Hagen and I had climbed trees together as children, though he had always been the more daring. But my time with dragons had cured me of fearing heights, and I made steady progress now, up through the canopy of trees and out into the sun, where I pushed aside the needlelike branches to look around.

Nothing. Nothing but trees and trees and more trees, where there were not mountains. Closer now than I had been before, I could see that beneath the trees that grew on them in patches the mountains were oddly regular in shape. They were conical, and black where there was no vegetation. In these spots there were holes or fissures, and smoke rose from them. I wondered if there were people or dragons living there after all, or if it really was poisonous gas like the Boiling Sea. It seemed remarkable that trees should grow so close to these vents of steam.

Other billows of smoke or steam could be seen rising out of the trees. It wasn't woodsmoke, it was too white. And smoke from dragonfire had a bluish color. As I squinted, trying to discern what it was, a dragon rose out of the midst of a large column of it, circled once, and then flew off a ways to land in the trees to the south. Another dragon flew up from the cloud, circled, and went east. Then a dragon rose out of the trees a league or so from the smoke, with something large and brown in its claws. A deer? A human? I wasn't sure at this distance. It circled the smoke once, then landed in it.

The circling meant something. It was a signal, or a ritual of some kind. There was something special there, where that great billow of smoke rose out of the trees. Something like a "lesser temple," I hoped.

I leaned out of my tree, fixing the angle of that column of smoke in my mind. It was a straight shot from the back left corner of my dragon's house. I thought that I could walk it in a day, if nothing impeded me. My only concern was that the thick trees might cause me to veer off course without realizing it. But I could always climb another tree and check my bearing.

Thinking about this, I didn't notice the sound of wings coming up behind me until my dragon swooped around and stared me in the eye.

"What are you doing?"

Not being able to answer, I only smiled and began to climb down.

On the ground I found another dead deer, and watched in disgust as the dragon ate it raw. He offered me a haunch, and I shook my head vehemently.

"You must eat," he said.

I mimed skinning it, although it made my stomach churn, and then roasting it with dragonfire. He looked mystified, but not because he couldn't understand. They had had cooking fires in the village, but apparently his personal servants had to make do with whatever scraps he threw them.

But not *this klgaosh*, by Jylla's golden braid! I pointed imperiously at the haunch, lying on the hard-packed earth between us, and mimed fire again.

Looking disgruntled, he ripped the skin off with one careless claw and charred the meat with a lick of flame. I gathered some large leaves off a strange plant to use as plates, laid them out, then shifted the meat to it and scraped off the charred part as best I could. The flesh underneath was barely cooked, but it was good enough, considering my ravenous hunger and the lack of anything better.

When I was done I gathered up the whole mess and threw it into the refuse pit along with the remains of the dragon's dinner. I tossed lime over it, and washed up in the stream. The entire time, the dragon watched me with half-lidded eyes, as though he had never seen a human behave this way before.

Judging by all the bowing at the village, and the disgusting state of his home, he probably never had. A human who yelled at him, who climbed trees, and who wanted things to be clean? No, I was a different type of *klgaosh* for certain.

I slept that night on the still-musty pallet, only a few paces from the dragon. I wouldn't have been able to sleep at all if I hadn't been so exhausted. I had slept near dragons before, but those had been dragons I knew: Shardas, Feniul, Velika. Dragons that I had felt were watching over me, keeping me safe in the night.

This dragon was a different matter. How long would he keep me here? Until I died of old age or from eating bad food? I could try to sneak out, but where would I go? Toward the column of smoke, I supposed, but there was no telling what I would find there. Besides which, he was lying across the length of the house, blocking the only door. I was caught, and didn't know what to do next.

Pine-Needle Tea

My dragon had a visitor the next day.

Another dragon, like enough to Darrym to give me a brief start, appeared in the clearing early the next morning. I was just blearily rubbing my eyes and wishing my mouth didn't taste so horrible when we heard the sound of wings and a roar of greeting.

"Bring *glark*," my dragon ordered, and went out to meet his guest.

I followed him. "What?"

Both dragons looked at me in surprise and irritation. I made a confused face and did the best I could to say *glark*, which had to be said with a huff of air and a sort of growl at the end.

My dragon's sigh steamed the bark right off a nearby tree. He turned to his guest and said something too rapid for me to really follow, but the gist of it was that I was hopeless as a *klgaosh*. Then he led me into the house and showed me a large pot, a sieve, and a canister of what looked like pine needles.

"Make *glark*," he ordered again.

I hauled everything outside while the dragons watched.

There was a fire pit in the clearing, and I found some lengths of chopped wood stacked against a tree nearby. I prepared the fire; then my dragon ignited it. I shook pine needles into the pot until the dragons nodded at me, before filling it with water. Since dragonfire is hotter than regular fire, the wood burned quickly and I had to scramble to keep adding wood. But the water boiled faster, too, and soon I was using the sieve to strain out the needles and running back inside for two large buckets for them to drink out of.

Once I offered them the drinks, they looked at me pointedly until I took the hint and left.

Around the back of the house I looked into the forest in the direction of that tempting column of smoke. The trees were very thick, but I found it reassuring. No dragon would be able to follow me on foot through that, nor would they be able to espy me from above.

I was close to fleeing. It was better than catering to the needs of this demanding, seriously unkempt dragon. But I had not eaten since the day before, and had no idea what plants around me were edible, so instead I planned.

I would need food: I wondered if I could take some meat and dry it to preserve it. How long did that take? If that wasn't possible, I should at least make sure my next meal was well cooked, and wrap what I didn't eat in leaves and hide it. I wouldn't need water; there were plenty of streams running through the forest. The dragon didn't seem to care about the canister of rice, so that had probably been intended for human food. I could take that, but it would have to be cooked. Unless I ground it into flour and made some little cakes with it, which would keep well and be lighter to carry. I mulled this over for a time. It was cool at night, but there was nothing like a blanket or cloak to be found here, so I would have to grit my teeth and bear the cold.

It did occur to me that I should head back to shore and let my friends know that I was all right. But I was closer to that column of smoke, and it wouldn't hurt to investigate first, in case that was the lesser temple we were looking for. I made up my mind to grind the rice and make the cakes immediately, and see about having my next haunch of venison overcooked, and got to my feet.

As I brushed the dirt off my rear, I heard another dragon land in the clearing behind me, and let loose with a sigh of my own. Time to make more *glark*, I supposed. At least I would have an excuse to keep the fire built up. There was a mortar and pestle in the house; if I took care of the rice quickly, I could have the cakes ready and baked by this evening.

But when I stepped back into the clearing, I froze.

The new visitor was Darrym.

"Creel!"

Despite my dyed hair and skin, he recognized me at once. He roared with rage, coming toward me, and I fought down my own anger at seeing the traitor who had kidnapped Velika. But facing an angry dragon is never wise, so instead I turned and ran toward the column of smoke, food or no food.

I had no other choice.

A Column of Smoke

I had been right about the thickness of the forest preventing pursuit: Darrym screamed his rage and even burned a few trees in my wake, but couldn't come after me. I crashed my way through the underbrush and leaped over fallen logs. As I ran, I sent up a prayer of thanks that I was wearing trousers and boots.

Once I thought I had gotten far enough away, I slowed down and tried to be quieter. Slipping between the bushes rather than crashing through them I also cut down on the trail I left. I felt like I was going in the right direction, but I didn't dare check by climbing a tree. At least, not yet.

Ullalal and her daughters had been right, I reflected, feeling the corners of my mouth turn up in a bitter smile. I had been a terrible choice for a *klgaosh*. If their dragon had chosen the youngest daughter instead of me, he and his friends would be sitting around their buckets of steaming *glark*, gossiping about how clever Darrym had been to capture Velika.

The thought wiped even a trace of a smile from my face, and I continued my grim march through the forest. I heard no noise of pursuit now, and I stopped and held my breath, straining for the sound of dragon claws, dragon wings, or dragon breath like a bellows. There was nothing, only the usual forest noises of birds and insects.

I found a good tree and began to climb, pausing just before I raised my head out of the forest canopy so that I could listen again. Again there was nothing, and I climbed up and out.

It was easy to find the column of smoke. It was closer now, and the air was very clear today, making it stand out starkly against the blue sky. Again I saw dragons making a single circle around it and then coming or going. There were more arriving, and with an intake of breath I recognized Darrym as one of them.

It was a place of importance; I knew it now for certain. Darrym had gone to report my presence, or to check on Velika, I could feel it to the soles of my feet. I ducked back down under the concealing leaves, and practically slid down the trunk of the tree in my haste. I needed to get to that spot as soon as possible, and it was still a good distance away.

I was fortunate enough to find some berries that I recognized along the way. With greedy delight I ate handfuls of them. Then I picked the rest and put them inside my tunic, using my sash to keep them in place.

Back home the berries would have long since been lost to frost if they hadn't been harvested, but the seasons were different here, on the other side of the world. During the day it was warm and misty like springtime, something that I felt even more grateful for than I was for the berries. It would be cold at night, but I still didn't have to worry about freezing to death, or leaving tracks in the snow as I escaped, and the smoke I was searching for would have been lost against a gray sky.

Well after dark, as I was staggering with exhaustion and thinking that I needed to stop soon, I saw the first sign that I was close. A squat stone pillar, carved with strange shapes that were menacingly unclear in the darkness, loomed before me. I shuddered, but kept on walking with renewed strength. There was another pillar, and another. And now there were strange, pinkish-flamed torches on poles, lighting a path through the forest.

I followed them, but not directly. Instead, I lurked in the trees and walked parallel to the path. Other paths met with the torch-lit one, the first of any paths I had seen in the forest. My heart beat as rapidly as it had earlier, when I had been running from Darrym.

My concentration was so completely on trying not to stumble over hidden roots while still keeping alongside the lighted path that I stepped into a clearing without realizing what I had done. The sudden glare of the pink torches combining with the moonlight made me blink stupidly; then I leaped backward into the concealing trees.

Peering out from the underbrush, I saw with relief that there had been no one to witness my sudden arrival and subsequent disappearance. But still I waited in the bushes, letting my eyes adjust to the difference between the darkness around me and the light before me.

What I saw as the clearing came into focus wasn't anything that I had been expecting. There was no house of wood or stone, no cave, no structure at all. There was a clearing, encircled by the torches with their pinkish gold flames, and in the center was the pillar of smoke, as wide as a large dragon and so straight that it was hard to imagine it wasn't solid. Dimly, where the smoke met the ground, I could see the ragged edge of a rift. The dragons were flying down into the earth, then. So that was where I would need to go as well. If Velika wasn't down there, and I strongly believed that she was, then at the least the dragons responsible for her abduction were.

But first I sat in the bushes and ate the rest of the berries I'd found earlier. The berries tasted strange, and I worried for a moment that they really weren't yellowberries, as I had thought. But then I noticed that the smoke from the torches had a peculiar odor, which was affecting my sense of taste. It wasn't the smell of dragonfire, or not quite, nor was it the smell of the Boiling Sea, back in Feravel. It was something else, something that smelled like rotting leaves and stone and rust at the same time. I hoped it wasn't unsafe for a human to breathe. It certainly smelled like it might be.

It seemed as though the dragons were gone for the night, or perhaps they were below, sleeping. I could face that risk, but didn't want to run into Darrym or any of his cronies as I was climbing down into the rift.

When the berries were gone and my eyelids were starting to droop, I slapped myself, got to my feet, and crossed the clearing. Standing at the edge, I looked down into the mouth of hell.

There were flecks and particles of ash in the smoke, and it stung my nose and nearly brought the berries I'd eaten back up. The rocky edges of the rift into the earth were hot and covered in powdery ash, which made the climb all the more treacherous. I told myself firmly that Velika was waiting for me at the bottom, and went down.

And down and down and down, and my legs were shaking and my arms were shaking, and I kept losing my grip and nearly falling. Looking around, I could see only more smoke and bright orange light that burned my eyes, and hear a roaring that rattled my teeth and was not made by man or dragon. I didn't bother to look again, I just kept climbing.

The cliff wall curved away from the rift, and for a while I think I was nearly upside down. I definitely didn't try to look around then, just offered prayer after prayer to the Triunity, and even a few blasphemous prayers to Tobin's Moralienin ancestors and the First Fires, on which the dragons swore. Someone had to help me, I thought, growing hysterical. I was on a rescue mission, after all, and if I didn't reach the ground soon my arms would give out and I would fall to my death. . . .

Just as the trembling in my arms reached the point where I could no longer hold on, my right foot hit solid ground. I collapsed like a rag doll onto a rough, porous rock floor and breathed in and out, in and out, savoring the feeling of not dying.

Then, as if it were being dragged from some poor creature's throat by force, I heard my name.

"Creeeeeel?"

I flipped over onto my stomach and squinted through the smoke. I was at one side of a huge underground cavern, the rough, black walls lit by a river of orange fire that flowed through the center of the chamber. It was from this that the column of smoke rose up into the rift.

On the opposite side of the river, lying on a raised dais of wood padded with leaves and branches, lay Velika.

The Queen on Her Throne

I scrambled to my feet and ran toward her, an embarrassing rush of tears flooding down my cheeks. I had to stop at the edge of the river of molten rock, teetering and feeling the heat wash over me.

"Velika," I said when I had composed myself, "are you all right?" My gaze went to her belly and I could almost count the eggs, they were so prominent.

"I . . . cannot . . ." Her words were drawn out, almost painfully so. "Drugged," she said finally.

"Drugged?" I strained to look through the smoke that separated us, searching for something, some food, water, whatever it was they were giving her, but there was nothing there. Only smoke and rock and the bed she was lying on. My hands were shaking again, now from terror and not exhaustion. How long did they intend to keep her drugged? Would it hurt the eggs? How was I supposed to get her out of here if she was too weak to fly?

"Are the eggs all right?"

"Yeesss." Her eyes kept closing, but I could tell that she was trying to listen to me as I paced along the edge of the river and dithered.

"How soon will you . . . lay . . . them?"

"Soon."

This made me pace harder. How soon was soon? Tonight? Tomorrow night? Next week? We had to get her out of here. I'd have to climb back out immediately and find Shardas.

"Can you try not to take the potion or what-have-you? Can you pretend to swallow, then spit it out?"

"No, she can't," said Darrym.

I whirled around. He was coming out of a narrow tunnel in the far wall, one that I hadn't even noticed through the haze. Without further warning he lunged forward and snatched me in his claws. Arrowing up and out of the rift above us, he didn't even circle once, just dove back down again into another hole in the ground, dropped me on the rock floor, and left.

"That is the second time a dragon has done that to me," I gasped, trying to get my wind back. "And I don't like it!"

"Creel?"

It was muffled, but the voice was unmistakable.

"*Hagen?*"

"Creel!" His voice was louder, and the frantic scraping sound that accompanied it made my teeth hurt.

A chunk of rock low down on the wall broke free and skittered across the floor. Through the hole it left I could see a human hand, dusty and scraped. It withdrew, and was replaced by Hagen's face, also dusty and scraped, peering up at me.

I crouched down and touched his face. "What are you doing here?"

"We were looking for you, of course," he said, looking not

the least bit nonplussed by our situation. "What happened to you? Shardas and Luka are frantic; they said you just disappeared."

"I got captured by some 'hoarded humans,'" I told him, rushing to get my words out. We needed to work on an escape plan. "They took me to their village, and then their dragon made me his personal servant. But Darrym came to visit and recognized me. So I ran off and found this place, and saw Velika. Then Darrym caught me and dropped me down here." I paused for breath. "You said 'we.' Who's with you?"

"Leontes." Hagen's head disappeared, and then I saw one of Leontes's green eyes peering at me.

"Hello, young Creel," he rumbled.

"Hello, Leontes," I said. "Can you fly out of your cave?"

"No, there's an iron grill over the opening. We are trying to dig through to your chamber, instead. I don't know if you saw, but there is a whole row of caves here, apparently for this very purpose, but the wall seems thinnest between our two chambers."

"Can I do anything?"

"Just stand clear. Now that we've broken through, it shouldn't take long."

And with that he curled a long foreclaw around the edge of the hole and began to tug. More pieces of rock broke off, and I could hear the horrible scraping again as he used his other claws to weaken the wall around it.

In a few minutes he had made a hole large enough for Hagen to climb through, and my brother gave me a rib-cracking hug. Then he handed me a jagged chunk of rock and showed me where to chip away at the wall. Side by side we went at it, while in the other cave Leontes did his part with rather more success.

Every so often, a shadow would pass across the cave entrances far above us. Hagen would leap back to Leontes and we would all feign sleep until the sentry went away again. We were lucky in that they hardly glanced at us, so certain were they that we would not be able to get out.

Until Darrym came.

This time Hagen had crouched in the ever-widening hole between our caves when a dragon's shadow passed over us. At my low signal, he went all the way back to Leontes, who let out a disgruntled huff at being interrupted yet again. Darrym crouched at the mouth of the cave and peered down at me.

"We needed the queen," he said, but there was no hint of apology in his tone.

"Why couldn't you just tell her about your people?" I had to shout to be heard; it was like being at the bottom of a well. "She and Shardas would have come to visit you! Why did you need to steal her?"

"We are the true people," he said, haughty. "We require the queen's presence. Those other dragons, with whom you have made *friends*"—he said the word as though it disgusted him to contemplate—"are blasphemers and fools. She should not be in such company."

"So she should be kept imprisoned?"

"Until she sees the true way," Darrym said easily.

"And if she doesn't?"

"Her eggs will be laid soon."

I could only gape at this. Did he honestly think Velika—
and Shardas!—would let them keep even one of the eggs?
They would die first! But perhaps that was the plan . . . if
Velika did not see "the true way." And what did *that* mean?
Keeping people as servants? Living in squalor?

"She belongs here with us, but a human could never
understand," Darrym said, his voice dismissive.

"Try to explain it," I said with gritted teeth.

At the same time, though, I wanted him to go away so
that we could keep digging a Leontes-sized hole in the wall.
We had to get out of here, to escape and save Velika, but
Darrym's horrifyingly matter-of-fact tone mesmerized me.
What was the reasoning behind this madness?

Darrym settled himself firmly on the edge of the pit and
drew a deep breath, preparatory to explaining. Beside me, in
the hole, I heard Hagen give a little moan of impatience, but
out of the corner of my eye I could see Leontes straining to
listen to Darrym, an expression of deep interest in his eyes.

"We are the chosen ones, those who followed the true
queen many generations ago," Darrym said. "It grieves us to
come to this, stealing away one who descended from the
false queen, but a female of lesser royal blood is better than
none at all."

"What under the Triunity are you talking about?"

Glaring down at me, and not needing my outburst to
continue, Darrym went on.

• "The granddaughter of the first queen had two daughters
of her own, born of the same egg," he said. "Mystics divined
that it was Aurania who was to be queen, but some of us

believed that this was not so. Her sister, Verania, was wiser, and so our ancestors followed her into exile here, on the far side of the world. But now Verania's daughter's daughter's daughter's daughter has died, and we have no one to bless us. We decided to bring the false queen here to help us, because her blood is still royal, even if it derives from the lesser sister."

"I see," was all I could say.

Darrym snorted as though he didn't believe that a human ever could see what he was talking about. But I did understand: twins, hatched from the same egg, had created a rift between two factions of dragons. And these were the remainders of the losing side, I supposed. Their numbers diminished, and their queen was dead. So they went after what they considered the next best thing.

Velika.

"Now, why are you here?" Darrym's muddy brown eyes stared into mine.

"To rescue my friend Velika," I said boldly. "From you."

"Impudence!"

"Oh, really? Let me remind you that when we first met, Master Darrym, you were lying on the Citatian shore with a collar around your neck pretending to be wounded so that you wouldn't have to fight! Shardas himself uncollared you, I helped you to find a home with Shardas and Velika, and this is how you repay us? If I am impudent, what are you?"

Another snort, and a flap of wings as Darrym flew away without answering my questions.

"He's gone," I told Leontes when the sound of Darrym's wings had faded.

"This is too much to digest immediately," the alchemist replied. "I must ponder his story as I scrape at the rock."

"I agree."

In silence we tore away the rest of the wall, and in silence we waited for night to fall. Once it was dark, Hagen and I mounted Leontes's broad shoulder and soared into the night sky, circled the column of smoke once to prevent detection, and went to tell Shardas what we had found.

Spears of Black Glass

Never do that again!"

If I'd thought that Hagen's earlier hugging was bone-breaking, it was nothing compared to what I got from Luka when we reached our camp. He practically dragged me off Leontes's neck, but I didn't mind. I was already leaping to meet him as the dragon touched the sand. We both squeezed each other and kissed and swore never to be parted again (and in Luka's case, occasionally just swore).

"I didn't mean to be captured," I told him, when I could breathe.

"But it does seem to happen to you with some frequency," Shardas put in. He came forward and whuffed at my clothes to reassure himself that I was all right.

"Twice is not 'some frequency,'" I said, my cheeks blazing. "And I've gotten myself free both times, thank you very much."

"With a dragon's help," Luka pointed out, and I gave him a quelling look, so he squeezed my waist again.

"And now the dragons need our help," I said, leaning against Luka's side. "We have to get Velika out of there. They're keeping her sedated, and if she doesn't come to accept living here and being their queen, they're going to keep the hatchlings and train them to do what they want."

Shardas barely managed to turn his head away before he let loose a burst of blue flame. It turned a long streak of sand to our right into a smooth glass plate.

Letting go of Luka, I went to stand beside the king of the dragons. I regretted blurting out what I had learned in that way, but Shardas needed to know. I put one hand on his fore-claw, drawing his angry blue gaze down to myself.

"We will rescue her and the eggs. We will."

"She's right," Leontes said. "I've seen where they're keeping Velika, and I have gotten a good count of the dragons that frequent that area. We can do this, Shardas."

"How? When?"

I had never seen Shardas so frustrated, so helpless.

"We'll go tomorrow night, after Hagen has helped me to prepare some mixtures," Leontes declared. "And in the meantime, I need you and my dear mate to make us some long spears of glass."

"Glass?" I wasn't the only one who said it with a look of disbelief.

"This sand will make very hard, very sharp glass, as we've just witnessed," Leontes said, pointing to the smooth slab Shardas had just unintentionally made. "It will come in handy for what I have in mind."

Shardas gave him a suspicious look. "Are you certain that you aren't just trying to occupy me with useless chores?"

"Quite." Leontes paused. "Some of the others might help as well."

Smoke still coming from his nostrils, Shardas finally turned and designated some glassmakers, taking them over to a large patch of particularly rough sand. Meanwhile, Luka, Hagen, and I followed Leontes up the ridge of rock to where he had set up his working space.

"Is it just a meaningless task?" I asked.

"Oh, no. We really will use them. But it has the added benefit of keeping Shardas busy," Leontes admitted cheerfully. "They will no doubt make far more glass than we could ever possibly use."

"Is this the first time that dragons will carry weapons into battle?" Luka picked up a strange brass instrument and studied it.

"Yes," Leontes said, taking the thing away from him and setting it carefully into the leather-bound chest with his other tools. "And it will also be the first time that dragons have gone into battle against one another without coercion. Which is why I must make medicine now."

This effectively silenced us, and we spent the next few hours fetching and carrying. We brought driftwood for Leontes to burn in a little fire pit with the smoke screened through a blanket. We brought him the scraggly moss that grew in the crevices of the rocky islet, and shells that had washed up on shore. At Niva's urging, we also brought him some freshly caught and grilled fish to eat, though he grumbled at the interruption. Things were ground, boiled, mixed, pounded, strained, and steeped until well after dark.

The next day I spent most of my time down on the beach with Shardas and the other glassmakers. Luka wouldn't let me out of his sight, something that I appreciated, but at the same time it prevented me from working on my wedding gown. I kept it by my side, though, in its basket, almost as a good-luck charm more than anything else.

As far as I could tell, there were already more glass spears than anyone would know how to deal with, and yet Shardas and the others continued to make them. Stack after stack of the rough, lumpy things lay on the beach, and there were now great pits where the sand had been hardened and dug up.

It was fascinating to watch, though.

Laying their muzzles parallel to the sand, the dragons would each send out a long, narrow lick of flame. The sand would melt and then harden into a lightning bolt of black glass. A dragon would scoop it up, run its claws over it to snap off any stray obtrusions and brush off the extra sand, and lay it carefully on the pile.

The stack of glass spears bothered me, though I tried not to show it. Instead I admired the look of the melting sand, and the fine fire control of the dragons. I didn't want to think about my friends using weapons against their own kind, even if the other dragons had kidnapped Velika.

Luka came up beside me, and I took his hand. "I want another look at that map that you and Leontes drew," he said. He, too, was staring at the pile of spears with a faintly alarmed expression.

"All right." I stretched up and gave him a kiss.

"Aren't you coming with me?"

I smiled at him, hoping that it wasn't as goofy-looking an

expression as I felt. It was just so strange and wonderful for him to be so . . . *worried* about me.

"Luka, I'm with Shardas, and Niva, and half a dozen other dragons I've known for years. I'll be just fine." I felt my smile turn more mischievous. "Besides, I can't stop fidgeting, and I absolutely have to work on my wedding gown."

"All right." Another kiss and he reluctantly left.

I turned around to find Shardas watching us, and blushed.

"He loves you very much," the king of the dragons said.

"I know. And I love him."

"You will be very happy together," Shardas told me. "And I will see to it, personally, that you do not encounter such difficulties as Velika and I have faced." His eyes clouded, and he turned and shot a jet of flame that made a longer, thicker spear than the others. He picked it up with a quick swipe, hefted it, and set it near his tail, where it could be easily reached.

"I think that's enough spears," I said, awkward.

"There will never be enough," Shardas said. "Never enough to ensure that Velika is brought safely home."

A River of Molten Rock

Leontes and Shardas had discussed using an illusion to disguise the rescue party as local dragons. But it was off-putting to look over at your friends and see them small and brown even if the trees far above were being pushed aside by their real height. And looking down at oneself and seeing claws that were unfamiliar would make for clumsy movements and awkward throws. No, for a mission of this delicacy, it was better to get the job done without alchemy, so the force that set out in the darkness was certainly impressive: jewel-toned scales, muted by moonlight, flashing on dragons the size of houses carrying long, black spears in their foreclaws.

I rode on Shardas, Luka on Niva, and Hagen was on Leontes. Feniul brought up the rear. We had all our gear with us, strapped down as tightly as it could be, and anything that wasn't essential had been dumped. Once we got Velika free we would signal to Amacarin, who was in command of the rest of our force. They would spread out over the forest to guard us against any pursuit until we were safely on our way back over the ocean.

Crouched low on Shardas's neck, I gazed down at the moonlit forest and tried not to let my worry overwhelm me.

If we got Velika free, how would we carry her out of there? The crevice that led to her underground chamber was hardly wide enough to fit a large dragon, let alone one supporting another, and she would be lethargic from the drug they were giving her.

Still, we would have to find a way.

We swooped low over the treetops, following the pink torchlight that showed the way to the underground chamber. It wasn't visible until you were nearly on top of it, so I felt the jolt as one of Shardas's spears caught in a tree and he had to drag it free. All around us, spoiling our silent, menacing entrance, were the sounds of tails and spears snagging trees, and even the occasional murmured curse.

But then we were there, with the ring of pink torches lighting the clearing beneath us, and the rift in the ground plainly visible not only because of the torches and the moonlight, but also because of the orange glow from deep below.

"That's it," I said to Shardas, unnecessarily.

Clasping the spears tight, he arrowed down into the crevice. We were both blinded by the smoke, and I counted to five before calling for him to halt, not wanting to find myself plunged into the river of molten rock or smashed on the floor.

He backwinged, bringing us out of the smoke and to one side about two man-heights from the floor. Leontes, Niva, and Feniul came down after us, crowding the chamber despite its size. I calculated that about a dozen local dragons could fit inside it, but with four of my friends, there was not enough room to spread their wings. They all began to drop to the floor, careful of the river of lava, and of Velika, who lay on her rustic couch, shuddering.

"Velika!" I kicked at Shardas's neck as though he were a horse, urging him toward her.

Something was wrong: her sides heaved and her tail beat an anxious tattoo on the rough stone floor. Her eyes were shut and her jaws clenched with pain.

"What's happening?"

"The eggs!" Shardas's voice was full of anguish. "Our eggs!"

Leontes leaped over the burning rift in the floor and rushed to Velika's side, Hagen clinging white-faced to his neck. Niva was on his heels, after sending Feniul back to the surface to order the others to stand guard. She crouched at Velika's head and began a soothing croon. Did dragons have midwives? If so, I couldn't imagine a better pair than an alchemist and a no-nonsense female with a clutch of children of her own.

But Shardas did not go to his mate's side. Shardas sagged there, on the wrong side of the burning river, and stared. The black glass spears clattered to the rock floor, and a terrible keening cry broke from him.

I swung down from his neck. "What's wrong?"

"We cannot move her now," he moaned. "She, and the eggs, will have to stay here."

I looked at him, then at Velika, then at Luka, who had climbed down from Niva and come to stand beside me. I twisted the ends of my sash. We couldn't leave her here; there had to be a way to get her to safety.

"A net?" My voice was a squeak. "You could carry her out in a net, couldn't you?"

"Absolutely not," Niva barked. "Leave the poor thing alone to have her clutch!" She looked daggers at Shardas. "And you: get over here and comfort her. Now."

When Niva used that tone of voice, you obeyed, whether you were the king of the dragons or not. Shardas lifted me over the rift, and then hopped over himself. He went to Velika's head, stroking her brow and murmuring to her, and Niva took up position near the queen's foreclaws, holding them tightly. Hagen, Luka, and I stood there, not certain what we should do.

"Well," Luka said, clearing his throat. "Er."

"How long until she and the babies can be moved?" Hagen asked the most useful question. "And how long until they hatch, anyway?"

"Three months until they hatch," said Leontes, and we humans groaned. "But they can be moved before then. In two weeks or so."

"Two weeks?" I frowned. "Why not now? What difference will two weeks make?"

"The eggs will not be hard when they come out," Leontes said. "But in two weeks they will be like the thickest stoneware."

"Like stoneware? Hardly!" Darrym came out of the passage at the back of the chamber, the one that I had once again failed to watch. "Moving them would be murder at any stage! They are more delicate than birds' eggs."

Leontes gave him an arch look. "It seems that you suffer from the brittle-egg sickness, as well as your other problems, then."

"Brittle-egg sickness?" Darrym's strut faltered at that.

Leontes waved a claw at the noxious cloud of smoke. "I suspect that the gases from the volcanoes may be causing some of your difficulties."

"Her eggs will really be as hard as stoneware?" Darrym sounded almost wistful.

"Yes!" Shardas turned on him, blue eyes burning. "So when two weeks are over I will take my mate and our eggs far from here."

"We need the queen," Darrym said flatly, recovering his arrogance.

"*You had her!*" Shardas roared. "We freed you from Krashath! You had a home with us on the Far Isles, and we counted you as a friend! Velika and I would have helped you all, if only you had asked!"

The queen stirred, moaning at Shardas's enraged roar, but he didn't stop. He stepped away from her, facing Darrym across the river of molten rock, and I could see trails of steam rising from his nostrils: his fire was burning high.

"We are the chosen people," Darrym insisted. "We followed the true queen."

"Well, you betrayed *her*, too," I snarled at him. Both Darrym and Shardas looked at me in surprise, and I wondered if they'd forgotten that there were even humans in the room. "She chose your ancestors to follow her, not her sister, and now you're 'settling' for her sister's great-great-granddaughter.

You've betrayed your own beliefs, as well as betraying the drag-ons who rescued you when you were collared." Hagen's influ-ence clearly got to me at that point, because I spat at Darrym, something I hadn't done since leaving Carlieff Town. Out of the corner of my eye, I saw Luka and Hagen exchange proud looks.

Whatever answer Darrym might have given to that was cut off by a tremendous groan from Velika. We all turned to comfort her as the first of her eggs arrived to the sound of Leontes and Niva humming in the floor-vibrating yet sooth-ing dragon way.

It was large, bigger than my arms could embrace, and did look soft, like a hard-boiled hen's egg that had been peeled. But it wasn't white, it was golden and glistening and beauti-ful, and I could see a curled form very faintly within it, twitch-ing as though startled by what had just happened. Leontes piled the more pliant, less prickly boughs around its base, so that the egg wouldn't roll away.

Darrym, hooting with excitement, started to leap the rift to join us, but Luka picked up one of Shardas's discarded spears. Bracing it against a dip in the rock, he squared off against the dull green and brown dragon. Hagen, too, lifted a spear as best he could, and set it. If Darrym jumped, he would be impaled.

"You may stay where you are," Luka said firmly, "if you won't leave them entirely in peace. But you have caused the king and queen enough grief, and will not interfere in this."

I felt a glow of pride in my breast, seeing their fierce stance. Figuring that the boys could handle the situation with

Darrym, I went to see if there was anything I could do to help. Velika's eyes were open the merest slit, and I thought that I saw them lock on me. So I took up a position by her head, with Shardas, and gently rubbed one of her brow ridges.

"You have a beautiful egg," I told her.

"Two!" The triumphant shout was from Leontes, and Shardas made a sound that was half cheer, half groan.

"Two," Velika rasped faintly.

"Don't worry," I told her. "We're going to stay here and protect you, and when your eggs have hardened, we're going to take you out of here. No more drugs." I raised my voice on this last sentence, hoping that Darrym would hear me.

The local dragons might outnumber us—I wasn't really sure. And they did have countless humans at their beck and call. But we surrounded Velika here in the chamber, as well as having dozens of dragons waiting above. We would care for her until she and her eggs could be moved, and then we would leave this horrible place.

Muttering all these things to Velika, I continued to stroke her brow through the birth of all eight eggs. Shardas looked as though he might faint, and Leontes was positively glowing with delight. Niva firmly declared it a successful clutching, and ordered Darrym to bring water and food for Velika. Immediately.

Darrym went, but he was rigid with anger at being sent to do Niva's bidding. Leontes, once he had seen to all the eggs, flew up to the rift to make the grand announcement, and I thought the roaring that followed would bring the ceiling down on us.

When the traitor returned, bearing a charred piece of meat and a bucket of water, he had a strangely satisfied expression on his face. Niva noticed it when she leaped the burning river to take them from him, and gave a sharp look at the tunnel behind him.

"Where does that lead to?"

But Darrym didn't answer.

"Leontes!" Niva shouted for her mate at the same time that I shouted Shardas's name.

"Block the entrances," Shardas bellowed. He picked up a claw full of spears, jumped the river, and drove three glass spears into the rock floor in front of the tunnel opening, creating a gate.

Niva did the same with the larger hole above us, flying up with her claws full of black glass to barricade the main entrance. Leontes just had time to squeeze himself through, turning in midair to help his mate. Through the black bars, I could see Feniul's anxious green face, calling out to ask what was going on.

"Who did you tell? What have you done?" Shardas snatched Darrym by the throat and heaved him off the ground.

Gasping, Darrym shook his head as best he could. Despite the fact that he was now trapped in a cave with four dragons who didn't like him one whit, he refused to answer. Shardas stalked over to the river of molten rock and held Darrym above it, forcing the smaller dragon to lift his tail high, lest it be burned.

"You told your people? How many of them are there? How are your human . . . slaves . . . armed? Tell me. Now."

No answer.

"I dived into the Boiling Sea of Feravel to save Velika's life," Shardas said. "We nearly died. Hot as it was, however, it cannot hold a candle to the heat of actual volcanic lava."

"We number fifty," Darrym blurted out. "And we have roughly a thousand humans. Bows and arrows, flint-tipped spears. I told our High Elder. He'll be mustering everyone to fight you, right now."

"Very well." Shardas tossed Darrym aside and crossed back over to Velika. "We can defend this cave easily," he told her. Now that she had eaten and drunk, she was looking more alert than I had yet seen her. Additionally, Leontes had given her a strengthening potion. "They will not dare to harm you and the eggs."

"Just leave us the eggs," Darrym pleaded, crouched in the corner. "We need only the first-hatched female; we'll send the others back to you."

"Darrym," Shardas said, "one more word and I'll dip you headfirst into the lava."

Taking Yourself Hostage

So, we're inside a volcano?" I gave the heaving river of fire a dubious look. "Isn't that dangerous?"

"We're some distance away, actually," Leontes reassured me. "I believe that the conical mountain to the west of here is the actual volcano. This is a tributary of its lava flow. A great many of the poisonous gases normally associated with volcanoes have already been vented, as has some of the heat."

"Not all of it," Hagen said, wiping his forehead with his sleeve.

It was true. Now that we were settled in, with nothing to do but wait, the heat was oppressive. Sweat ran freely down our faces and necks, and we had removed our boots and stockings. Even the dragons were starting to look uncomfortable, shifting about and rearranging the piles of branches and leaves unnecessarily.

I leaned back against Luka with a sigh. "Are you sure that you want to marry me?" I let my eyelids droop. "I keep leading you off on these dangerous missions, and I'm too backward to even know what lava looks like."

He settled an arm around me. "Well, you are very troublesome, but at least you're concerned enough about your education to travel so far just to see lava in person," he replied.

"If you two get all mushy, can I leave?" Hagen mimed being sick.

"Where exactly were you going to go?" I ignored the fake gagging.

"I thought I might go see where that tunnel leads," he said. "The glass spears are far enough apart that a human could slip through."

I looked beyond my brother at the tunnel entrance. It was true; a human *could* squeeze between them. Which meant that we could go out . . . and a local person could come in.

Niva, listening idly to our conversation, seemed to come to the same conclusion. She snatched up more spears, and we all went over to the tunnel mouth. Without thinking, I turned sideways and slipped through, and Luka followed me.

"What are you doing?" Niva whispered as well as a dragon could. "You don't know what is waiting at the other end."

"We're armed," Luka said, patting the hilt of his sword. I had only a belt knife, but I knew how to use it. "Come along, Hagen."

"What? No!" I tried to push my brother back through the gap.

Luka put a hand on my arm. "Creel, we need his help."

I squinched up my eyes for a moment and then nodded. "All right, but stay behind us."

"Yes, captain," Hagen said, and saluted me.

We edged our way down the dark tunnel until it made a

sharp bend. Peering around the corner, we could see a large opening, filled with light.

"I'm still all dyed dark," I whispered. "I'll go."

My tunic and skin were muddy brown and my hair was coal black. In the back of my mind, I was worried that it wouldn't wash out in time for the wedding, and I would have to get married looking like a spun-sugar figurine that had gotten too close to a candle.

Back to the wall, I sidled along the passage until I came to the opening. Hiding behind a rough spur of rock, I peeped into the chamber beyond.

There were a number of humans kneeling in a circle around what looked like a pile of old furniture. And then I realized that it was quite simply the oldest dragon I had ever seen. His flesh hung off his bones and his scales were so dry they looked like dead leaves. His eyes were milky white: blind. His voice sounded like the hiss from a teakettle.

I wasn't fluent in the dragon tongue, and this dragon's voice was harder to understand than most. But one of the kneeling men had a map, and I could clearly see the rift over our heads marked on it. The man was moving pebbles around the map, apparently following the instructions of the dragon. There was a cluster of bluish pebbles with a ring of gray ones around them. The man moved the gray ring in closer to the bluish cluster.

It didn't take a keen understanding of the language to translate that. Our friends on the surface were surrounded and about to be attacked.

I slithered back to Hagen and Luka. Pulling their hands,

I led them quickly back down the tunnel and into the safety of our barricaded cave. Niva pounded more black spears into place, sealing the passage against human or dragon intrusion.

"I need you to fly me up to the main entrance," I told her. "We've got to warn the others. The locals are coming; they have or are about to surround Feniul and the others and attack them."

Niva snatched me in her claws and we took off, coughing as we flew through the column of smoke. It clouded her vision enough that she hit her head on the spears blocking the entrance, and nearly tossed me right out through them with the sudden change in speed.

Feniul stared back through the bars at me as we regained our composure. "By the First Fires! Are you trying to kill yourselves? How are Velika and the eggs?"

"Feniul!" I flapped my hands at him, ignoring his questions. "You have to get out of here! Fly away, right now, all of you! The locals are massing all around, ready to fight."

"They are? Oh, my! I had better find Amacarin." He lashed his tail and clacked his foreclaws together nervously, then stopped and gave me an uncharacteristically steely look. "No, Creel. We won't leave the queen undefended."

"That's very noble, Feniul," Niva said in her dry way. "But I really think it best that you all go. Better to wait until you have the advantage, and then attack. You're about to be ambushed, and I can't see that it will do anyone any good."

"I will not leave Velika and Shardas," he said.

"Fine, but at least give the others the option to leave, and quickly."

Feniul turned and began shouting that they were being surrounded, which made Niva and me wince. So much for secrecy and having the ambushers leap into an empty clearing.

And, of course, that is precisely when the ambush came: while our friends were milling around, debating whether they should go or stay. I screamed for them to stop. I even yelled that they could have an egg if they withdrew, but no one was listening to me. Niva and I could only watch as the battle unfolded above us.

A Compromise of Sorts

Being underneath a battle is just as terrifying as being in one, I soon found. Particularly if you are friends with some of the participants, and even more particularly if they are fighting over your fate.

Niva should have flown us down where we wouldn't be accidentally burned or struck by a stray arrow, but she couldn't look away and neither could I. After their shouts for information went unanswered, Leontes flew up with Hagen and Luka, and we all stared up in horror.

The noise was the worst part.

I had heard dragons roar in rage and in battle, so that was nothing. It was the humans that began to get to me. Making a screeching sound that went on and on as though they never needed to take a breath, the dragon-collected people of this land raced to and fro, screaming like birds of prey and shooting our dragons with frightening accuracy. Though their arrows were tipped only with stone heads, they pierced dragon scale when the aim was true and, added to that, the local dragons flamed and clawed with little care for the safety of the human fighters.

An arrow shot through the bars that separated us from

the fight, and Leontes caught it in his foreclaws. He was carrying Hagen and Luka on his back, while I still huddled in a basket made of Niva's foreclaws. The alchemist dragon studied the tip of the arrow with a frown, sniffing at it and scraping it delicately with one claw.

"This is dragonglass," he said after the inspection. "Not stone. It's no wonder it can go right through a scale. And it's either poisoned or drugged, I can't tell. Not a mixture that I've seen before."

Niva let out a jet of flame as an enemy dragon leaped over us. She grinned with triumph when he howled and flew upward to nurse his wounds out of the fray. "Poisoned? We have to bring an end to this!"

"Take me down," I told her. "No one up there is listening to us."

"Don't you want to see what happens?" Hagen's eyes were too bright, as though he weren't certain whether to be excited or appalled by his first sight of a battle.

"I want to *stop* what's happening," I said. "Take me down."

"Yes," Luka said, and I could see that he, too, was riveted by the battle. "Perhaps if Shardas ordered the fighting to stop. Or if Velika could fly up here."

"No, keep them away from this." I drew back a little as some flame licked between the bars from the other side. "I'll stop it."

"How?" Luka's full attention was on me now, and I saw his brows draw together in worry. "What are you going to do?"

"I'm going to have Niva move those spears again, and I'm going to go down that tunnel and talk to that old dragon."

Luka groaned, but slapped Leontes's neck. "You'd better take us, too," he said.

"She's not going alone," Hagen agreed.

"I wouldn't mind the help," I admitted as Niva turned and glided back down through the smoke.

When we landed, we saw that Velika was sleeping, curled carefully around her eggs. Shardas left off hovering over her to join us by the tunnel entrance, and we quickly told him what was happening.

"I forbid it," he rumbled. "I'll go up there and stop that fight right now."

"You're more likely to get caught by a stray arrow," I said, and Leontes and Niva nodded.

"Or," Leontes put in, "someone will realize who you are and do it deliberately."

Darrym, huddled in a corner, raised his head. Shardas snarled at him and the traitor hid his head under one wing.

Pulling free another of the spears that blocked the tunnel, Shardas said, "Then I'll speak to this aged dragon myself."

"You won't fit," I said, my voice kind. I put a hand on his foreleg. "Shardas, let me try to negotiate a peace. It will be all right."

Everyone held their breath for a moment, but in the end Shardas nodded. Luka, Hagen, and I slipped between the remaining spears and crept down the hall. Behind us we could hear Shardas and Niva disputing the danger he would be under if he went to observe the battle.

The boys crowded my heels as we went around the bend

and hesitated by the outcropping of rock that half-hid the doorway. In the chamber beyond we could see the elderly dragon but there were fewer humans gathered around him.

"We can't speak dragon," Hagen whispered in my ear.

"We'll do the best we can," I said. "Perhaps we can get one of the humans to follow us back to our cave, and they can speak to Shardas directly."

"Is this our best plan?" Luka squeezed my hand.

"Do you have a better one?"

"I'm afraid not."

"In we go, then!"

Still holding Luka's hand, I stepped forward into the light. I thought we would make a dramatic entrance, but only the dragon was facing us, and he was blind. After a moment, Hagen coughed nervously, and all the humans whirled around to stare at us in varying degrees of horror and surprise.

I just looked back at them, and then beyond them to the dragon. I really had never seen a creature so old. I don't think he could have moved from his couch if he had wanted to. Despite his blindness, his head was tilted as though he were looking back at me.

"Do you speak Feravelan?" I asked loudly and clearly.

Nothing from the humans or the dragons.

"Roulaini? Citatian?"

Still nothing.

I took matters into my own hands, literally. The nearest human was a young woman, perhaps a year or two older than I. She was festooned with beads and bangles, and her loose, black hair hung nearly to her knees. I stretched out my free hand, grasped her by the upper arm, and tugged.

"You will come and talk to Shardas, the king of the dragons," I told her.

She shook her head violently, pleading over her shoulder with the dragon, or possibly her fellow servants. Some of the words she used sounded almost like a human equivalent of the dragon language, and that made me even more determined to drag her along.

The elderly dragon raised its head a bit more, and said something imperative in the native tongue. The girl stopped squealing, and began sobbing quietly, boneless in my grip. I looked at Luka, shrugged, and then we led her to the dragon king.

"I thought *you* were going to negotiate the peace," Shardas said with amusement when we thrust the weeping girl through the spear barricade. "This works just as well, I suppose."

And then he began, speaking to the girl at great length and gesturing frequently at Velika. The girl wouldn't even look at the dragon queen or her clutch. After one sidelong glance at Velika's reclining form, the girl fell to her knees with a whimper. She responded to Shardas's words with monosyllables, but didn't look at him either.

"I could never live like this," I whispered to Luka.

"No," he agreed. "I've seen you try to grovel. It's not very convincing."

I flicked his shoulder with my finger.

Finally the girl got unsteadily to her feet and went back to the tunnel. I felt rather useless, but I followed her all the same, with Luka at my side. Hagen stayed behind, and Leontes said he would take him to observe the battle.

The girl reported what Shardas had said, or so we hoped. Then she listened to the elderly dragon's reply and we returned to Shardas, who heard her out, his face grave.

"This elder is their default leader, since the death of the last royal female," Shardas explained to us. "He says that all our friends must leave, right away, or be killed."

"That's not going to happen," I said, crossing my arms. I glared at the girl as if these were her orders.

"And I have explained this," Shardas continued. "They wish Velika to order everyone to leave, but I doubt she will have much success either." He cocked his head to one side. "They seem to have regarded their queens as deities. I'm not sure that he understands that our friends could refuse her orders."

"So they keep humans as slaves, and were in turn slaves to the queen?" Luka's eyebrows climbed to his hairline. "That sounds . . . rigid."

"To say the least." Then Shardas breathed out a sulfurous gust of air and began the task of explaining the unlikelihood of anyone simply stopping the fight and leaving the country just because Velika said so.

The girl took off before we could follow, so Luka and I waited with Shardas. She was gone a long time, and then a wheezing in the passageway drew our attention to it.

It wasn't the girl returning, it was the elderly dragon, come to meet this unusual queen and her mate himself. Shardas grabbed the glass spears and wrenched them from the ground to lay them aside.

Scales rattling, breath coughing its way in and hissing its way out, the dragon tottered out into the chamber with humans on each side to guide it. Darrym came quickly over and spoke to the elder with low urgency, but was dismissed with an airy wave of one emaciated foreclaw.

That almost made me like the aged beast.

The elder was helped to the edge of the lava, and then stopped there. I didn't know how they expected to get him across, and I could tell that Shardas didn't want him any closer to Velika. All of my friends hopped across to stand around the sleeping queen, taking Luka, Hagen, and me with them. Darrym tried to follow again, but a look from Shardas made him stand near the elderly dragon with a falsely casual air instead.

Shardas gently woke Velika, and she looked at the elder dragon gravely. Then she greeted him, with great respect, but without uncoiling her tail from around her eggs. He answered with equal respect, straining forward, his nostrils working as his other senses tried to get a picture of her that his eyes could not.

And then Velika did a very clever thing.

She reared back her head, looming over the blind old dragon and his attendants, and gave him a direct order.

"Stop this battle at once. Leave us in peace. Now." Her voice was regal, commanding, everything they could want in a queen, and I turned expectantly to the elder one, waiting for him to comply.

Dragon voices are like rocks tumbling together, but this dragon was so old that his sounded more like sand being poured over stone. Still, his resolve was clear: he would not stop this fight, not even for the queen.

Velika's tone was anguished, and the dragons in the room gave a general gasp of horror at her next words.

"What did she say?" I grabbed at Niva's foreclaw. "What was it?" I had caught only a few words.

Niva's voice shook. "She will crush her eggs rather than let them hatch in this place if he doesn't comply."

Now, belatedly, the humans gasped, and I looked to see that Velika's powerful tail was flexing around her fragile eggs. I started toward the eggs, my hands outstretched, but Niva stopped me with the same claw I had been clutching.

Everyone stopped. Stopped moving, stopped breathing, stopped speaking.

Then the sand-over-stone voice of the elder dragon came again, to the agitation of his attendants. Velika's tail relaxed, but only slightly, and Niva breathed a huge sigh of relief.

Darrym took the girl we had commandeered as a translator in his claws, and flew her up to the opening of the chamber high above us. He bellowed, and when the battle above quieted a little, she shouted something that brought all the fighting to a halt.

"Is it over?" I hardly dared to whisper. "Can we leave now?"

"No," Niva said, sounding relieved yet still wary. "The fighting will stop, our friends may stay. But—"

"But?"

"But they still expect to keep Velika and our eggs," Shardas said.

Sand Poured over Stone

As the eggs hardened, we grew ever more restless and anxious. The locals, both human and dragon, knew that we wanted to take Velika and her eggs and leave, and they were determined that that wouldn't happen.

While the eldest dragon, whose name was Mannyl, returned to his lair, he left Darrym to keep watch. Other local dragons came and went, until Velika announced that they were bothering her and must be banned. But apparently not even the queen could ban Darrym, whose smugness made me want to slap him until his scales flew off.

Fortunately, with the uneasy compromise came some amenities. Food, for one thing, and water, for another. There was also rough bedding for us humans, which made things a little easier.

It was quite boring to sit in the hot, smoky chamber day after day and simply stew, however. Shardas and Leontes took turns teaching us the dragon language, partly as a way to pass the time, and partly so that we could better understand the locals. From time to time I would hide on the far side of Velika's bulk and work on my wedding gown. Hagen and Luka would practice fighting: Luka taught Hagen to use a sword, and Hagen taught him how to box like a Carlieff Town local, which involved a lot of shouted insults and the occasional head butt.

And then at last the eggs were hard.

Shiny and opalescent, they gleamed with the reflected orange fire of the nearby lava. Shardas and Velika hovered over them with proud concern, feeling for any weak spots, and we spoke in low voices about what to do next. Darrym tried to listen in; he even asked quite politely if he could touch one of the eggs, but Shardas told him that if he came any closer, he would find himself missing a tail.

"We can arrange some sort of carrier," I said quietly. "A basket. Or a net."

"Then we'll just have to burst out of here," Shardas said, not entirely rejecting the idea. "And outrun the guards."

"They don't harass our friends above," Niva mused. "But if they saw us trying to escape with the eggs, they would be sure to follow even if they didn't dare to attack."

"There can be no true escape," Velika said. "We must find a solution for all of us. If we run, they will hunt us, and we shall never have a moment's peace."

"But they will not back down from their position," Shardas reminded her. "Either you will rule them, and them alone, or we must wait until one of the eggs hatches and give them the firstborn female." His claws clasped gently around one of the eggs in an unconscious gesture of protection.

"They must be made to see that if they truly accept my sovereignty, they must let me go free and rule them from our home," Velika said crisply. "And if what Leontes suspects is true—if it is the fumes from the volcanoes that are causing them to die off—then they should come to the Far Isles anyway."

"But they've lived here for centuries," Hagen pointed out. "Why are they only getting sick now?"

"The volcanoes were dormant until a century ago," Leontes said. "The brown female who brings our meals told me. Many of their homes were destroyed or made unlivable by the smoke and lava, just in the last few decades."

"Then they *must* come with us," Velika said firmly.

"You would really let your captors live with you in the Far Isles?" I stared at her in astonishment. I was not that forgiving.

"I am their queen," Velika said with simple majesty.

"But, ma'am, how do we convince them to come?" Luka shook his head thoughtfully. He had his arm loosely around my waist, and I squeezed the hand that rested on my hip. "For all their awe of you, they don't even seem to think that you have a will of your own."

"They must be made to see," Velika repeated. "Somehow."

"Well, I need some fresh air," I said. "Perhaps Luka and Niva and I could go up to the jungle, and talk to our friends for a bit." I made a slight jab with my chin in Darrym's direction.

"Yes," Shardas agreed.

He and Niva flew up to the opening of the cavern high above and began removing the spears of glass that still blocked the entrance. It made us all feel safe to leave them there, and so Feniul had been passing us food and sharing news through the barrier.

When they had removed enough to allow Niva to pass through, Luka and I gathered a few things and prepared to mount the huge, green dragon. I didn't even notice that Darrym was gone until he came back out of the tunnel with Mannyl, the elder dragon, on his heels.

The sound of the elder's voice was mesmerizing. The steady *rush*, *rush*, *scrape*, *grate* caused me to gaze at the pitted scales of his muzzle without blinking until Hagen nudged me.

"Are you paying attention?"

"What?" I blinked sleepily at my brother. "I only understood one word in three."

"Then you *really* should be paying better attention," Hagen said. "He's saying that none of us can leave."

"Wait! What? He is?"

My little brother nodded, certainty in the grim set of his mouth. Hagen and Leontes had been spending a great deal of time together, and it seemed that Hagen's mastery of the dragon language had surpassed mine by leaps and bounds.

I focused on Mannyl's words, instead of on the sound of sand on rock, and heard him repeat what he had just said. He did not like the idea of us going up there. It was not "safe."

Snorting loudly, I turned to Velika. "Perhaps it is time to remind him who the queen is," I said to her.

"Exactly."

She loomed over the smaller, older dragon, and in no uncertain terms let him know that she needed her friends to go up to the surface.

If the elder's voice had been a gentle fall of sand before,

now that he was angry it was a torrent, a landslide. The sound filled my head and made my teeth shiver as if I were biting into a piece of ice.

Velika bared her fangs, and fire glowed in her mouth as though she were barely keeping herself from blasting Mannyl to oblivion. "By the First Fires, you shall not order me like some slave!"

Her words were clear even with my limited knowledge of dragontalk.

And so was Mannyl's reply, for there was no mistaking the reaction. Through the newly opened entrance in the cavern roof, summoned by the grating, rushing shout of their elder, came ten strange dragons.

They filled the cavern, eyes hard and breath even more sulfurous as it combined with the fumes from the river of fire. Before we could react, they were upon us. Luka was seized, and Hagen. Two each took on Niva and Leontes, throwing nets around their heads and wings so that they could not open their mouths or fly away.

To my shame, my sense of self-preservation kicked in, and I leaped backward to crouch among the eggs, sure that they would not risk harm to them. Velika spread one wing over the eggs and, from its concealment, I peeped out, watching in horror as my betrothed, my brother, and two of my dragon friends were hauled off like baggage.

I tried to jump up, to follow them, but it was too late. Velika's wing was like a roof of iron over my head, and the eggs hemmed me in on every side. I could only watch, and curse.

When they had gone, she released me, and I went to stand beside Shardas. He put a claw out, and I held on to it, tightly. Then he turned to Darrym.

"You will leave. Now. And never come within my sight again." Shardas's voice was hard.

Darrym sneered back. "I will go when my elder tells me to."

"You will leave this place, as my consort says, or I will kill you myself." The hardness in Velika's voice sent chills down my spine, and I took a little step farther away from her.

Darrym, too, looked chilled. And then he flew up and out of the cavern without looking back. It was a dragon we had never seen before who came to replace the missing spears above us with alchemically treated logs and to stand guard so that we knew there was no chance of escape.

Into the Jungle

We did have the benefit now of being able to speak without being heard. The catch was that there were only Shardas, Velika, and myself to plan what to do next.

Shardas hovered near the opening in the ceiling for a while, trying to catch sight of our friends. After a time he glided down to report that neither a familiar dragon nor a familiar human could be seen now, only the silent sentry.

"That doesn't mean that they have been harmed," Shardas said, trying to soothe both Velika and me.

"But it still isn't good," I replied, though not rudely. "We have to reckon how to get out of here. All of us."

"It's clear that they don't truly believe in my sovereignty," Velika said. "They want a queen, but a queen that they can control. A figurehead to worship from a distance." She shook her head. "It makes one wonder what the last queen was like."

"That's true," I agreed. "All the dragons I've met here have been so . . . bossy. With their human slaves worshipping them, and the way they even order *you* about."

"Little more than a slave herself, is my guess," said Shardas. "No doubt they kept her in fine style: food, human servants, every luxury their primitive land offers. Why should she argue?"

Shuddering, Velika began to stroke and turn the eggs. She had been carefully rotating them every few hours since they had been clutched, to ensure that there were no flat spots on them. If an egg was flat anywhere, I had learned, there was a chance that the hatchling would be malformed.

I wondered if lack of turning was also at fault for the mean stature and dull coloring of the local dragons. If they did have the brittle-egg sickness, they might be too delicate to turn over.

"We're not leaving any of the eggs here," I said resolutely. But this had been said many times since the clutching, so I went on. "We must either convince them to let Velika and all the eggs go free, or we must destroy them."

This last had not been said, at least not aloud, though I suspected that much of Shardas's muttering had been to this effect. But now that it was out in the open, we all paused for a time to consider it.

"Kill them all?" Velika closed her eyes. "Could we do such a thing, and live with ourselves?"

Tail lashing, Shardas looked ready to insist that he could, but then he sagged. "I do not wish to harm anyone," he admitted. "Unless forced."

"But perhaps," Velika said softly, "perhaps if some were convinced to take our part. Those that oppose us could be captured. . . ."

"We'll need to know how many sympathize," I said, trying to look at it sensibly, to imagine that it could be done.

"If we could talk to Niva," Shardas said, and now his tail was lashing again, but with frustration, "she could get this all sorted out in a matter of days."

With my head thrown back until it made my neck hurt, I looked at the logs that covered the opening of the cavern above us. No dragon could get out of that, and it would be only too obvious if one did. But a small human, on the other hand . . .

"I'll do it," I said, stopping Shardas in his tracks. "I'll sneak out tonight, find the others, and send them to talk to the locals. Maybe some of the humans will join our cause as well. They can't enjoy being cowed this way."

We waited until nightfall, and then Shardas flew me up to the entrance. There was a dragon standing guard, but I was dressed in dark clothes, and I don't think she was watching for a single human to slip out. She didn't even glance my way as I slithered through the barrier and crept across the clearing to the cover of the forest.

Finding the path that I had come to the underground temple on, I again followed it from within the trees, keeping out of sight. A trio of humans came up the path near dawn, carrying baskets of food, and I hesitated, wondering if I should approach them. But they looked eager to deliver breakfast to the sentry dragon, laughing and chatting, and so I waited until they were well away before I continued on.

I didn't want to end up back at the home of my "dragon master," though I was headed that way. But if I went beyond his house, I knew that I would be approaching the shore, and that was the best way I could think of to contact our friends.

I was hoping beyond hope that Luka and Hagen had simply been dumped on the shore, and that they weren't languishing in a dungeon somewhere . . . or worse.

It did occur to me that by stopping off at my old master's house, I might see Darrym and manage to overhear some gossip about them, but I would also run the risk of getting caught.

So when I reckoned that I was near that dragon's home, I veered away. I raced across the path, and began walking parallel to it on the other side. It was full light now, though very little really filtered down through the leafy canopy. In the green twilight I climbed over fallen logs and stumbled over moss-covered rocks. I was quickly losing my impetus, and wishing that I had eaten more before I had left.

I was quite caught up in imagining what I should have eaten, and so stumbling into the yard in front of a large dragon house came as something of a shock.

Even worse, the dragon was just coming outside, and saw me at once. We stared at each other for a long time.

The Arrangement

I started to back into the jungle, but the dragon halted me with a barked command. I turned it over in my head: I had improved my knowledge of their language in the past weeks after all. She was asking if I had a message for her, clearly believing me to be a servant for one of her neighbors.

Smiling as disarmingly as I could, I shook my head and held out my hands in a helpless gesture.

The morning light betrayed me, though. My clothing, my skin and hair showing pale through the fading dye, my blue eyes—all stood out far too brightly in the sunlight, and I knew it.

She pounced on me like a cat and took me into her house, setting me down in the middle of the floor. This house was considerably larger and much cleaner than that of the dragon I had served. Along one wall were several piles of fresh bedding, leading me to think that she shared the home with a mate perhaps, and children.

This made me uneasy—how many dragons would I be facing when the others returned? I counted at least four beds. But it also gave me a rather wider audience than I had planned on, if I wanted to convert some of the locals to our cause.

"You are the girl with the *others*?" the dragon asked, studying me closely.

"Yes, with Queen Velika," I replied simply in Feravelan.

She glared and ordered me in dragon: "Don't say that name!"

I bit my lip, not wanting to antagonize her any more than I already had.

"Where is my son?"

The question startled me even more than stepping out of the trees into her yard had. Her son? Who was her son? I thought of Darrym visiting my one-time dragon master, not that far from here. Was one of them her son? But I hadn't seen my master since I had fled his clearing, and Darrym should have been back by now, unless . . .

Then it hit me: the little dragon we had captured, Darrym's younger brother. She must mean him! He was still being held out on the rocky islet where we had made camp. At least, I thought he was. I racked my brain, trying to think of his name, and remembered that he had none: he wasn't old enough to have human servants.

I plucked at a bit of gray cloth that lay on one of the dragon couches, raising my eyebrows, and then roughly sketched Peder No-People's dimensions in the air.

The mother dragon looked ready to roast me. "Take me to him."

I had to think this over for a moment. If I showed her where we were encamped, she could return with a war party and attack. On the other hand, she could fly me right to my friends without my having to tramp through miles of forest. And, with other dragons there to persuade her in her own language, it was possible that she would join our cause.

Although her older son *was* the odious Darrym.

Instead, I came up with a compromise of sorts. I would have her take me to the shore near some other islets, but close enough to ours for me to signal to my friends with a bonfire or something.

Nodding, I let her scoop me up again. I tried to ask if I could ride on her back, but she only blew smoke derisively at me. Carrying me in her foreclaws, she flew to the shore where I directed her.

I quickly gathered some driftwood and lit it with the flint in my belt pouch. We had never seen a human on the shore, so my friends would want to investigate immediately, I was sure.

They must have been on edge—of course they were!— and keeping a careful watch. The fire had just gotten going when a large form glided toward us.

Darrym's mother cowered: it was plain that she had never seen what I considered a normal-sized dragon before. And it was only Feniul, who was not extremely large when compared to Shardas and Niva.

But never had I been so glad to see Shardas's dear green-clawed cousin. I leaped to hug him around the neck as soon as he hit the sand, so overjoyed that I didn't even notice Luka until my betrothed slithered down from Feniul's back to hug me just as fiercely.

"I've been so worried about you! I've been frantic with

missing you!" He lifted me clear off the ground and I laid my cheek against his.

"You too!" It was a stupid thing to say, but it was all I could think of. "How did you get free?"

"They brought us here and dropped us," Luka explained. "I guess they didn't want to offend Velika by hurting her friends."

"Hagen? Leontes? Niva?"

"All well," Luka assured me.

"Thank the Triunity," I said.

"What happened to you?" Luka released me just enough to make certain that I wasn't injured. "What did they do?"

"Nothing. Velika and the others are fine. I snuck away," I said, glad that Darrym's mother couldn't understand us. "To see what had happened to you." I took a steadying breath. "And to tell you what we need to do."

"Before you go further, Creel, please tell me: what is this lady doing here?" Feniul darted a suspicious look at the female dragon.

Sudden exhaustion washed over me. How was I going to do this, really? How was I going to negotiate the release of the nameless young dragon, convince everyone to let Velika go free, and . . . I could have sworn there was something else I needed to do. I sagged against Luka, who picked me up and held me close to his chest.

"Just rest," Luka murmured. "You can't save the world all the time, you know."

Seeing that I was fading, Feniul turned to the dragon and

addressed her directly in their language. He seemed alarmed at what she had to say, though, and turned back to us at once.

"She wants her child back, which is understandable," he explained. "But as soon as he's free, she's threatening to tell everyone where we are and that we stole her son, which is worrisome, to say the least."

"She can't do that," I said, panicking a little.

"No, she can't," Luka agreed. "Tell her that if she wants to see her child, she has to promise not to reveal that we had captured him, or where we are camped."

"Even better," I said, sitting up in Luka's arms and causing him to quickly change his grip on my legs so that he didn't drop me. "Even better: tell her that if she wants to get him back, she has to meet us tomorrow with ten other dragons."

Both Feniul and Luka stared at me. Disbelief warred with concern on their faces as they patently came to the conclusion that I was suffering from some sort of brain fever.

"We need to convince these dragons that Velika cannot stay here and be their pet," I said. "They have to let her go, and all her eggs. I snuck out for two reasons: I wanted to make sure that you were all right"—I gave Luka's shoulders a squeeze—"and I wanted to see how many locals we could convert to our cause."

Feniul relayed our request to the female, but she violently disagreed. She wanted her son, she wanted him now, and she wanted to see us punished for our crime.

I could hardly blame her, so, with much arm waving and Feniul to translate, I told her that we had a special message from the queen, and needed to tell as many dragons as possible.

"Very well." She sniffed. "Bring my son to the southern temple," she told Feniul. "You will return him to me, and then the humans may speak to us. Or I will bring every dragon and human in our land against you."

A Wall of Scales

This is terrifying."

We were standing with Amacarin in the middle of the forest clearing where the southern temple of the dragons was located. The temple itself consisted mainly of pillars that marked a loose circle in the trees, and some stones set into the mossy ground in a pattern that looked as though it had a ritualistic purpose.

"Said the girl who once clung from Niva's neck, trying to get a collar on her. *Niva!*" Luka rolled his eyes. But his face was white and he was clutching my hand. "And then you leaped off a roof onto a strange dragon's back, shortly before jumping aboard several strange dragons in the middle of a battle."

"I spend a lot of time hanging too far off the ground," I commented, trying to sound brash but coming out high-pitched. "I should stop that."

"True. As soon as you do *this*." With his free hand Luka gestured at the crowd in front of us.

Like a wall of scales, fourteen local dragons stood in the clearing. And gathered around the dragons were their people. Hard, dark eyes stared at us. The white markings on their faces stood out starkly against their tanned skin, giving them the appearance of even greater hostility.

Taking a young dragon was a serious crime here, since hatchlings were so rare, and it looked more like we were on trial than anything else. My heart sank further as I saw my original captor, Ullalal, and her daughters standing beside the dragon I had served for that disastrous day and a half.

"I don't think I can do this." I tried to step back.

Luka let go of my hand, but only so he could push me gently forward. "You're the heroine of the Dragon Wars," he said. "I'm convinced that you can do anything."

This made me smile, and I was still smiling when Feniul landed beside us. He had the little, nameless dragon with him, and also Niva and the orange dragon Roginet.

"This is more than ten of them," Feniul hissed to me.

"I noticed."

"Be prepared to leap onto my back if we have to get away quickly," he said.

"Righto," Luka said.

Now that our dragons were here, it was time to begin. I took yet another step forward, seeing every set of eyes—human and dragon—follow my movements.

"As you all know," I began, "I am a friend of Queen Velika Azure-Wing, and I am authorized to speak for her today." I paused to let Feniul translate, and then waited a little longer to let my words sink in.

"Velika is very displeased. Her life and the lives of her mate and her eggs have been threatened." A number of the dragons looked shocked at this, and so did all of the humans.

I took heart: perhaps they didn't know what was going on down in that cavern and it was Mannyl alone who was corrupt, not the general population.

"She was stolen away from her mate and her friends only weeks before she had her clutch. The elder dragon who lives in the lesser temple has told her that she will not be allowed to leave, ever, unless she gives up one of her children."

More disbelief, shocked murmurs, head-shaking. Luka gave me a wink. We had their sympathy, I was sure of it.

Just as I was preparing to say more, Darrym's mother called out from the front of the crowd. She was standing as close as she could get to her younger son, who was still tethered to Niva on one side and Roginet on the other.

"We are the true people," she said. "We need the queen more than these vain, fancy dragons with you! She belongs to us!"

"Yes, she *is* your queen! Your queen: not your slave," I countered. "A queen is not kept in a hole in the ground, forced to do your will. The queen of the dragons needs to be free to go to all her people who need her. She is to look after the sick, bless matings and hatchlings, and guide you to fertile lands."

Niva, to one side, nodded approvingly. She had undertaken my education in the duties of the king and queen of the dragons last year, when it was revealed how little I knew about my friends' culture.

"But she is not the real queen," Darrym's mother shot right back. "As descendants of the First Mother's line, we have certain privileges."

This raised Niva's hackles too much for her to remain

silent. "You have no right to keep the queen in a dungeon!" Then she blasted the air with flame, a serious offense in a peaceable gathering of dragons.

Darrym's mother's insistence got to me, too. It reminded me too much of Mannyl and Darrym, so smug about kidnapping Velika and holding her prisoner, completely convinced as they were that whatever they did was right and good.

"If you are the chosen people," I said, and Feniul had to scramble to translate, breathing steam as he was from outrage, "why is it that your numbers have dwindled? Why has this very land turned against you, poisoning you with noxious smoke?" I stared around, making eye contact with all of the dragons that I could, willing them to think about what I was saying.

"Is it that you have displeased the First Mother? Keeping the queen locked away like this can only offend the First Mother more," I went on. "Velika is still descended from that first dragon, and is of royal blood. It is wrong of you to treat her this way. You must persuade your elders to set her free. Now that she knows about you, she will continue to aid you. But she must be free."

There. That was the meat of my argument. If it didn't work, it was back to sketching skirt patterns, as Marta would say. I hardly dared to look around, but when I did, I saw . . . understanding. Worry. Even shame, as they contemplated the seriousness of what they had done.

I caught Luka's eye, and we dared a small smile at each other. I quickly wiped mine away, though, not wanting to appear to be gloating. But as I turned my head, I saw Darrym's mother.

She did not look ashamed. She looked furious, her eyes filled with hatred.

And all of it was directed at me.

"Give me my youngling," she said, her voice cold.

"She doesn't like us," Luka murmured.

"No, she does not."

"How dare you accuse us of kidnapping, when you have held my youngling against his will so many days!" Darrym's mother said.

Feniul's chest puffed out. "He threatened the safety of the king and the queen. We merely kept him with us so that he could not endanger them. He was not harmed. He was well fed, well cared for."

As a point of fact, I noticed that little Peder No-People looked in fine spirits. He had been whispering back and forth amiably with Roginet this entire time, and he appeared to have gained weight during his captivity.

"I want my child," the mother dragon hissed.

"And Velika wants her children," I snapped back. "All of them. You'll get your wish. Will she get hers?"

This took even Darrym's mother aback, and I saw quite a few dragons hang their heads. I went over to the young dragon and freed him myself, making my movements broad and dramatic.

"You are free," I said loudly to the young dragon.

"Thank you," he said, looking rather sad. "I have to go

home now," he explained to Roginet and reluctantly went to his mother.

She fussed over him for some time, making sure that he wasn't injured, while he looked embarrassed. I raised my eyebrows at the orange dragon.

"A nice young fellow," Roginet said in his accented Feravelan. "Ze mother seems a bit odd, zough."

Luka coughed to hide his laughter.

One of the local dragons saw this, and came forward. "You have been among them?" He loomed over the young dragon, who lowered his head subserviently.

"Yes, noble Vannyn."

"Who is he, this king? What sort of creature is he?"

I held my breath, and Luka's hand, as all around us both species strained to hear the answer.

"He is . . . great, Noble One. Powerful, strong, and . . . good."

"Good?"

"Kind. And wise. He loves the queen very much." And if a dragon could have blushed, the nameless young dragon did.

This caused much clucking and murmuring from the other dragons, and the "Noble One" looked at me.

"We have never had a king," he explained. "Our queens' mates were always chosen for them, and they had no status among us."

Another piece of history from Niva rose to the forefront of my brain. Shaking my head as though facing a roomful of students, I said, "The First Mother herself chose a king for her oldest daughter and heir, but said that ever after, the queens must choose their own mates. The king was to be the leader in times of danger, she said, and no queen was complete without her king by her side. In the Dawn Days, Queen Rialta and her king, Nethem, were said to be of one voice and one heart."

"How can you know this?" Darrym's mother looked appalled when Feniul's translation sank in. *"How dare a human speak of such things?"*

The assembled humans were all averting their eyes from me, as though I had done something truly awful. Ullalal's face was a mask of horror, and the daughter who had envied my servitude had both hands over her mouth, as though she might be sick.

"The penalty for any human who speaks of sacred matters is death. Immediate death by burning," Darrym's mother said with great satisfaction.

"Is that true, or is it something you invented?" Niva asked with great disgust. "For I have never heard of such a thing, and I have known the queen since I was hatched."

"It is true," Vannyn, the Noble One, told us. "However, I do not think it applies to this young maiden, since she is not of our people." He gave me a reassuring look.

I tried to smile back, but I felt rather uneasy myself. Darrym's mother looked as though she were going to burn me to ashes right now, without further argument.

"Of course it does not apply," Feniul said. "There is no ban among our people on humans knowing the ancient legends. We should encourage it, really. There would be fewer wars and misunderstandings."

Dear Feniul. I did manage a smile for him, and Luka's grip on my hand relaxed a bit at the blunt sensibility of the green dragon's tone.

"Wars? With humans?" Darrym's mother looked down her nose. "Has this lesser queen fallen so far from the true way? Does she not control the humans among you?"

"Dragons do not own humans, not in any legend or law that I have ever heard," Niva said stiffly. "Again I say: is this truly the ancient way, or something that you have invented?"

Before Darrym's mother could retort, Vannyn spoke up.

"Perhaps it is a measure of how far we have fallen from the ancient ways," he said heavily. His gaze swept the assembled humans. "It is our vanity, and our shame, that we now keep slaves, something our ancestors would never have condoned. Nor would they have condoned the kidnapping of a queen . . . or any female! And the continued captivity, the threats of taking away her hatchlings, are an abomination."

I'm not certain who looked more surprised: me, Darrym's mother, or the humans who had just discovered that there was no need for them to be slaves.

Back in the Cavern

Encumbered by my heavy pack, I slipped between the logs blocking the entrance to the lesser temple with Luka right behind me. Shardas caught us easily on his back and carried us down to Velika. I had forgotten how hot and malodorous the molten river was, and hoped it wasn't affecting the health of the little dragonlets. We would need to get them out, soon.

After assuring the dragons of our well-being, and asking after theirs and the eggs', we related everything that had happened at the meeting, and the aftermath. It was quite a lot to tell, with Vannyn ultimately decrying the practice of keeping humans and the kidnapping of Velika with equal vehemence. The local dragons had divided into two camps: those who continued to believe in what they considered the old ways, and those who followed this Noble One.

It was a great surprise to Darrym's mother, but not to anyone else, when her younger son refused to go with her. He had taken a stand beside Roginet and announced his intention to follow the large, orange dragon wherever Roginet should lead.

In a terrible temper, his mother had at last flown off with

her supporters in tow. They consisted of four dragons—and no humans—which made their exit less dramatic than I'm sure she would have liked. Also remaining was my former master, and his people, who looked uncertain and were murmuring among themselves in low voices.

Vannyn had spoken at length to his people, urging them to remember the old stories. Never had humans been kept by dragons, not until well after the death of their first queen, who had started the schism with Velika's many-times-great-grandmother. If the dragon they considered their true queen had not condoned human slaves, who were they to do such a thing? Furthermore, who were they to order a queen about, holding her captive and shunning her chosen king?

Vannyn was an eloquent, passionate speaker, and I realized after a little while that I had tears silently sliding down my face. Luka saw them as well, and put his arms around me. Tucking my head against his shoulder, I whispered that it felt like we might win this battle at last.

But there was still much to be done. The Noble One sent his followers, human and dragon, into the jungle to spread the word, then sat and talked with us for a time. We shared our stories, relating the events of the Dragon Wars briefly, but also telling how we came here and what Velika's situation was now. He told us he was in fact one of the council of elders, but that his collection of humans was really just a village he kept an eye on. None of them had come to the meeting, because it was too far for them to walk, and he never carried humans around "like goat carcasses."

We all agreed that things needed to move quickly. He

had two days to win more converts to the cause while we watched over the queen. He would come to the cavern in two days' time, either to set us free with the blessing of the other elders, or to help us escape. We needed to be ready for either situation.

"What does that mean?" Velika fretted over her eggs. "How can we escape with the eggs? Shardas and I are too large to fit down that little tunnel, and the eggs are too large to be carried by a human."

"Oh, we'll have to fly out the main entrance," Luka said. He reached into his pack and pulled out a coil of rope. "But first we'll need to play with this."

I opened my own pack, and showed them that it was as full of blankets. Luka, in turn, took more and more rope out of his.

"It's for a net," I said. "We're going to pad it with blankets to carry the eggs in. *If* the local dragons won't agree to set us free. If they want to make peace, we can carry the eggs up one at a time and take them somewhere more comfortable. But if that old dragon won't release you, and Vannyn cannot convince the other elders, we will have to put the eggs in a net and make a run for it."

I smiled nervously. "It will be all right," I said, more for my own sake than for theirs.

"It will," Shardas agreed. "You have done great things, both of you. Let us take this rope across the lava, so that we can spread it out better."

When some of the human minions came to bring us a meal, they were startled to see Luka there. Startling too, I'm sure, was the bizarre way Shardas was sprawled across the floor.

After they left, we all looked at each other and started to laugh. Shardas got up and we went back to work, still snorting with laughter, on the ropes he had hidden with his bulk.

"It is tempting just to flame anyone or anything that gets in my way, you know," Shardas said confidentially, as I bent over a knot. "But Velika will not have it."

"And she's right," I said reprovingly. "That won't help bring 'round the locals here. Which you must do, unless you want to be fighting with them all your life," I reminded him.

"I know, and I don't want more war. But I've only just truly begun to act as a king again. And it is hard not to take my duties as leader and protector to heart."

"If someone kidnapped you, I'd kill them," Luka told me almost cheerfully. He threw down another coil of rope, and whistled as he wove it through the others.

"You're both incorrigible," I said, but I couldn't help feeling a little bit flattered.

Just a little.

I had never made a fishing net, but I had tatted little mesh purses, and this was much the same. Well, instead of a small copper tatting shuttle, I had a coil of rope draped over my shoulder. And our concern was less that we would lose our coins out the holes than that an egg would fall and smash, but it was essentially the same.

Or so I told myself as I ducked and skipped, using my entire body to weave the net, while Luka followed in my wake. He was pulling the ropes taut, and tying bits of twine around the intersections of warp and weft, so that the net wouldn't loosen at any key points. Shardas was using his bulk to hold down the ends of the ropes, plucking and tightening where directed, or cutting the heavy ropes with a swipe of his claws.

When the basic net had taken shape, we stopped to look over our work. A large square of rope mesh, just big enough to nestle the eight eggs, was spread before us. Next we would have to find a way to gather up the corners, and rig a harness for Velika. The ropes looked rough, and I worried that our coarse woolen blankets would not be enough to protect the eggs.

Velika leaped across the river to look at it.

"Ingenious," she murmured. "I am tempted to leave with the eggs as soon as you can finish this."

"We must give them the chance to make peace with us," Shardas said, as though he hadn't been considering an all-out battle himself only hours before.

"I suppose." Velika sighed. "Still, it will be reassuring to know that an escape is ready if we need it."

We checked the knots and then rolled the net up and hid it in Velika's bedding. We didn't want to risk our captors seeing the net when they brought us breakfast the next morning.

But there would be no time to dwell on that.

The River Rising

The next day we were awakened by bands of light shining down from the cavern entrance. Usually we were awakened by the scraping of the bars across the tunnel when they brought our food, but not so today. We blinked around groggily, and when no breakfast was forthcoming, we went to work on the net with our ears cocked for approaching footfalls.

It was Velika who finally noticed something truly amiss. She had been on the verge of hopping across the lava river to help us fit her to the harness, but stopped short and called out to Shardas.

"My love, come quickly!"

We had been busy on the far side of the cavern, all three of us with our backs to the lava. The heat was nearly unbearable, but it always was, and Luka and I had been running back and forth with coils of rope, until we were dripping with sweat anyway.

What we saw when we turned around made us perspire even more, however.

The river of lava was overflowing its banks, coming dangerously close to Velika and the eggs. She was pulling them clear with her tail, but even as we watched, a blob of molten rock spat out with a hiss and ignited some of the dry brush that formed her bed. She smothered it with a claw, and exchanged frantic looks with Shardas.

"The volcano," she said.

"It's erupting." Shardas finished the thought for her.

"Surely not," Luka said, trying to look calm despite the pallor coming over the red heat of his cheeks. "We would have heard more . . . rumblings or some such thing." He looked from one dragon to the other. "Wouldn't we?"

"I have felt them, deep within the mountain as I lay here, but assumed it was normal," Velika said.

"We're getting out of here," I announced, my voice shaking. "Right now, peace or no peace." I looked at the entrance to the tunnel. "Three guesses why they haven't brought us breakfast."

"You don't think they would leave the queen and her eggs?" Luka was aghast.

"Rats will flee from the scythe with or without their babies," I said dourly. It had been a saying of my father's. "And so, apparently, will the local dragons."

"But we won't," Shardas said firmly. "We shall bring the eggs across," he told Velika. "And lay them directly in the net."

"I'll get the padding ready," I said.

First we laid all our blankets atop the net; then Shardas brought over the dried boughs and rushes of Velika's bedding in huge clawfuls. We made the best nest that we could, and at last we were ready to load the eggs.

Holding the first one so delicately in his claws that it

looked like it might slip from his grip, Shardas carried the egg over the churning river of lava. He set it gently into the nest, and Luka and I packed more rushes around it to keep it from hitting against the next egg.

When all the eggs had been carried across, Velika stood above them and we set to work tying the net to her belly. Shardas had volunteered to do it himself, but we pointed out that we needed him to guard us.

Now he helped place the ropes for the harness over Velika's back, taking care that they wouldn't interfere with her wings. Luka and I ran about underneath her, adjusting the net and tying the ropes as Shardas passed them to us.

When we had knotted and tied and adjusted, Velika stood and took a few steps, testing the balance and strength of the carrier. My heart flew to my mouth as I heard two of the eggs knock together, and Velika went rigid with horror.

Emptying our packs, Luka and I burrowed into the net ourselves and shoved our spare clothing between the eggs. We even took off our tunics and sashes to add them to the ever-more-slapdash contraption, so that we were now in just our trousers, undershirts, and boots. By then the cavern was too hot for more clothes anyway.

Soon all we had left was the basket containing my wedding gown, which I fastened to Shardas's back before it, too, became a casualty of the situation.

Velika walked in a tight circle, the most she could manage in our increasingly small cavern. "It seems to be holding," she said, her voice concerned. "Thus far."

"It will have to do, until we get up to the surface at least,"

Luka said, looking at the lava river with anxiety. "We haven't much time left."

Shardas flew to the entrance above us and began to rip the logs from their moorings. We held our breath, both from the hot, strange smell of the lava, and from fear that our guards would try to stop him. But no one interfered, and Shardas ventured out into the clearing, returning a minute later with a bundle of glass spears held loosely in his foreclaws.

"There is no one above," he said. "They appear to have abandoned us." His lip curled at their cowardice, and I felt my own expression mirroring the dragon king's.

Luka and I climbed aboard Shardas, and he soared up to the entrance and out. Crouched on the edge of the rift that led to the cavern below, we looked around to see . . . nothing.

There were no guards, human or dragon. The torches had burned out, and from the forest there was only silence. No birds called, no wild goats bleated. All was still, save for a faint rumble that had been going on so long I only now noticed it. It was the volcano. At its tip I could see a glow, a brightness that pulsed in my eyes and stained my retinas.

"Velika, it is safe," Shardas called to his mate.

With a roar of defiance, she burst up through the opening and prepared to land heavily beside us.

There was a creaking and groaning, and then a *snap*. We looked on in horror as several of the ropes binding the net of eggs to Velika's belly separated. The net plunged to the mossy ground, and Shardas prostrated himself, dropping the spears and thrusting his foreclaws under the eggs to break their fall.

Luka and I leaped from Shardas's back to help. The eggs

appeared to be fine: they were tightly packed and their father had gotten his claws under them just in time.

Surveying the points where the harness had broken, I could see that it was the twine that had been the problem. The stress of Velika's movements, her powerful leap into the air, had made it unravel. I exchanged glances with Luka. Where would we get more twine? And what good would more do if it wasn't strong enough to take the strain of Velika's movements anyway?

Taking his foreclaws from under the net, Shardas too puzzled over the knots. "We need something stronger," he said hopelessly.

"And soon," Velika said softly.

The rumble of the mountain was growing louder, and the sky was darkening, not with clouds, but with smoke and ash from the volcano. We needed to fly, fast.

"We could carry the net between us," Shardas said.

"But if we are attacked," Velika argued, "what then? And the net itself may not hold. . . ."

"We can cut my shirt into strips," Luka offered. "And use it instead of twine."

"It's linen," I said. "It will unravel just as fast as that twine."

My heart was beating rapidly. My palms were wet and my mouth was dry. There was only one thing to do.

"Hand me your knife, please," I said to Luka, and my voice caught in my throat.

"What are you going to do?"

"It's sharper than mine." I pulled the basket down from Shardas's back.

"Creel!" Luka stared at me in shock, and Velika and Shardas both snorted smoke in consternation.

"Silk is stronger than most rope," I said, and laid my wedding gown on the ground. "We'll need strips about two inches wide, ten inches long."

"Creel, if we must . . ." Luka put an awkward hand on my shoulder. "I'll do it."

"No," I said, and the word came out as a sob. "I want to." I took his dagger and jabbed it through the heavy silk of the skirt of my wedding gown. Tears dripped down and spotted the fabric.

"It is . . . was . . . very fine," Shardas said comfortingly. "One of your best."

Velika rumbled warningly, and he backpedaled.

"Of course, you are very gifted, and can surely re-create it when we are safe," the dragon king assured me.

"We don't need the top part . . . the bodice," Luka pointed out in what he probably thought was a comforting way. "You can still use that."

"Of course." I sniffled, and made another cut.

A Hole in the Mountainside

White strips of silk, their ends fluttering, adorned the harness and net that Velika wore. White strips of silk that had once been a gown that I had begun to think of as my masterpiece. I continued to cry as I tied them around the weak joints of the ropes, but it had to be done.

Down below in the vent, we could see that the cavern floor was now entirely covered with lava. The ground shook, and fire began belching out the top of the mountain.

Our escape from the cavern would be pointless if we couldn't escape the greater threat of the volcano.

We were headed toward the shore, and our islet. It seemed that we would be able to get away without dealing with the local dragons after all, though I think we all feared they would still have to be faced.

We worried about our friends, as well. Having seen no sign of any other creature—dragon, human, or even bird—we were afraid that something might have happened to them. Were the locals using the eruption as a distraction in order to capture our friends? Had some other catastrophe occurred during the night, to which we had been oblivious in our cave underground?

But as we neared the shore something caught my attention, and I called out to Shardas. To the northeast was a mountain that we had previously seen only from the opposite side. Approaching it from this angle, though, we realized something looked odd. All the hills and mountains on this island were covered in trees, but this peak was bare. Too bare. With the exposed rocks making a pattern that seemed highly unnatural, even in this smoky light.

Shardas, curious as well, veered course to bring us just close enough to investigate. To our amazement, we saw that the barren place was actually a temple carved into the side of the mountain. The huge door could clearly accommodate dragons; in fact, it was large enough for two of the local dragons to fly in abreast.

Velika called out: "Don't even think about it, Shardas. I am not taking my eggs anywhere *near* there."

"Agreed," Shardas said, but I could tell his curiosity was still piqued, as was mine.

"Look there!" Luka pointed past my shoulder to the right, and I tapped Shardas's neck to indicate the direction.

A trio of small, brown dragons was flying toward the temple in an odd formation. Two of them flew side by side, so close their wings nearly touched, and the third was below them, wings outstretched and barely moving. On second glance, thin ropes could be seen running from the two higher dragons to the one below.

They were carrying the lower dragon in a sling.

It had to be Mannyl, the elder.

Velika heaved a huge sigh. "Let's land right there," she

said, pointing to a small open area in the forest below.
"Prince Luka can stay with me while you and Creel investigate."

Luka tried to protest, but Velika pointed out that even if
she kept me with her, I would find some way of involving
myself in something dangerous. It was therefore better for me
to be with Shardas from the beginning.

I found myself grinning abashedly at this summation of
my character. Velika knew me all too well. We landed lightly
in the jungle, and Luka and I thoroughly checked the eggs
and makeshift carrier.

It looked as though the pieces of my gown were fulfill-
ing their new purpose. The net and harness were holding
tight, and the eggs hadn't so much as shifted during the
journey.

Luka hugged me. "Thank you for giving up your gown,"
he said gruffly. "We'll get you another one, a better one."

"How?" I tried not to sound too heartbroken. After all,
what was one gown in the face of eight young dragons' lives?
"We'll be lucky if we make it out of here in time for the wedding at all."

"We can delay the wedding," Luka offered, and I hugged
him again.

"That won't be necessary," I assured him. "I'm sure that
Marta can whip something up. She probably already has a
replacement waiting: she was convinced something bad would
happen to this gown."

"Marta, Prophetess of the Triunity." Luka laughed.

"Come along, Creel," Shardas said gently. "Keep an eye

out for signs of the eruption. If you hear roaring, or if the forest starts to burn, flee," he instructed Velika and Luka.

"Right-o, sir," Luka said.

Velika didn't even reply.

I remounted Shardas and we headed straight for the temple. He didn't bother to conceal himself. . . . How could he? He was three times the size of the local dragons, and bright gold besides. We just flew brazenly to the entrance and passed through.

Into a place of wonder.

We were in a huge chamber, big enough to house a hundred dragons. The entire mountain must have been hollow, and there were ledges along the cavern walls for dragons to lounge on. Few of them were filled, though. Shardas quickly landed on one in a shadowy corner high above, and none of the dragons gathered seemed to notice.

What took my breath away, though, wasn't just the size of the chamber, but that every wall, every ledge and inch of floor and ceiling was carved with pictures portraying dragons. Dragons caring for eggs, young dragons frolicking, dragons fighting in battles, fishing in the ocean—everything you could imagine. The deep carvings were inlaid with gold and priceless stones, adding color and dimension to the images. The pink torchlight made the jeweled eyes and scales wink and glimmer, so that the carvings appeared to move.

I clenched my fists, wishing I had something to sketch designs on. These scenes would make the most fantastic patterns for a gown! I tried to drink in just the pictures on our ledge, but was interrupted by roaring.

It seemed that we hadn't entirely escaped notice after all.

"Do you want to stay here?" Shardas's claws clutched at the lip of the ledge.

"There's no way for me to get down if something happens to you," I said.

With that, Shardas soared to the floor far below with me still perched on his back. There was a ring inlaid in the stone that seemed to indicate a place of importance, and off to one side was a low couch containing the elder Mannyl. Another dragon crouched nearby, and I thought it was he who had raised the alarm. Glaring, I saw it was my old master, and Darrym was with him as well.

Settling himself elegantly in the ring, Shardas looked around, nodding at the other dragons. A king surveying his people, in truth as well as demeanor. I got down from his back as gracefully as I could, and stood by his side with clasped hands and smooth expression.

"So this is the Great Temple of the First Mother," Shardas said, his voice carrying to every ledge. "How very . . . ignoble of you to conceal it from your queen."

My smooth expression changed to shock and confusion. The Great Temple of the First Mother? The first *dragon*?

"If Velika had come into line, she would have been brought here," Darrym said arrogantly.

I wished heartily that Shardas hadn't left his spears with Velika.

"It would be very hard for her to 'come into line' if she had died in the cave where you left her," Shardas snarled. Gasps ran through the temple. "That's right," Shardas cried,

"Velika, our eggs, our human friends, and I were left in that cavern to die as the volcano erupted. We barely made it out in time!"

"The eggs?" The ancient dragon on his couch sniffed the air, searching for some sign of them despite his blindness.

"Are safe. Away from here," Shardas said.

"Good, good," Mannyl said. "We need them."

"Yes, you do," Shardas replied. "Because she is your queen and one day one of our hatchlings will succeed her." He glared around the room. "And you will treat my mate, and her heir, as your queen. Not as your captive."

A dragon came forward, and a smile stretched across my face. It was Vannyn, our greatest ally here.

He bowed his head graciously to Shardas. "My king, welcome to the Temple of the First Mother. Long has it been the shame of our people that we hid it from our brethren."

Hissing and snorts erupted at this, but not that many. Looking up, I saw many ashamed nods, and one dragon gave me a rather cheery wave. I waved back.

"He is the troublemaker, Elder One," Darrym said. "He has been stirring up dissent."

"I am the one who still has a shred of honor," Vannyn roared. "I am the only one not too blind to see that we are dying, rotting from within. Our lies, our cruelty, and our vanity have brought us to this!" He swept his tail around. "A handful of us left! Weak and sickly! Our eggs rarely hatching! Do you really still think we are the chosen people?"

"I never did," Mannyl said.

Silence filled the temple.

The Queen in the Ring

W hat?" Even Shardas was taken aback.

The elder's breath rattled in and out. I wasn't sure if it was a sigh or laughter, but it was chilling all the same. I had a sudden vision, too, of him dying before he could tell us what he meant.

"The answers are here, if you know where to look," he said finally. A feeble claw waved in the air. "But it would take you days to study all the carvings, months to interpret them. No one has done so in centuries. Except for me."

"You don't need to tell them anything," Darrym hissed, his voice frantic. Even if he didn't know the meaning of the carvings, I think he suspected what the Elder One was going to say.

I know I had my suspicions, which were causing little bubbles of excitement in my chest.

"Velika and her mate have won," Mannyl said. "Or so they think. The volcano is erupting, none of us may survive."

This burst my bubbles of anticipation, I must admit.

"Most of these carvings were done at the order of the First Mother herself," he continued. "But others were added by a later generation, after the majority of our people had left this land. Our beloved Queen Verania, she who called us select few the chosen people, had more carvings made and hidden around the temple.

"They tell the story of a jealous young dragon whose elder sister was favored by their mother, a great queen. Her mother, her father, those who attended her hatching all agreed: she did hatch second. In her jealousy, however, the younger dragon left her family behind and chose to make her own way: as a queen, surrounded by adoring followers as she had always longed to be.

"By great fortune she found this land, to which our people had long ago forgotten the way. It was the land of their ultimate ancestor, where the mother of us all had burst forth from the First Fires.

"She found the temple, and here made her home with her followers. But when she was dying, she felt great remorse, and recorded her confession. That is the truth of our beloved Verania." The aged dragon sagged back, gasping for air.

"Well," I said softly to Shardas, "I hardly expected that."

"Nor I," he admitted. He peered at the other dragons. "So. Now you have the truth: Velika *is* descended from the true queen—your line has always followed an impostor. What will you do?"

A ragged cheer went up, but mostly from those who already supported us. Many of the dragons shuffled their feet and looked ashamed, which was all well and good, except that it really didn't help us with the erupting volcano and the negotiation of peace between the two factions.

"They will help to gather the humans and bring them here to safety," Velika said crisply. She had soared into the temple and landed beside Shardas, her movements neat and grace-ful despite the burden of her eggs.

Luka slid from her back and came to stand beside me. I took his hand and squeezed it tight. "We couldn't bear the suspense," he whispered, through the rising tide of murmurs from the assembly.

"The queen!"

"She's here!"

"See how many eggs! And so large!"

"At last, a queen! At last!"

Velika scanned the crowd. "How many of you have human villages dependent upon you?"

I could see that her forthright question startled them, but they were quick to raise foreclaws. And every one of them seemed to have a hoard. That meant fifty villages at least, by my estimation.

"You must go, quickly, and start bringing your people here. Tell them to make haste, take nothing that will slow them down, and you must carry as many as you can. The old, the sick, the children."

"What? Humans here? Never!" Darrym bared his teeth. "It violates the temple to even have *them* here!" He waved disdainfully at me and Luka.

"The volcano is erupting," Velika said, "and the lava will overtake everything. We must save the humans! I believe that we will all be safe within the temple, but we must hurry if we are to do any good."

"There will always be more humans; they are a plague upon the land," Darrym sneered.

Shardas's tail lashed out and caught Darrym square in the jaw. The smaller dragon flew across the room and hit a pillar, collapsing in a daze.

"You heard your queen," Shardas roared. "Go!"

The dragon still crouched beside Mannyl shook his head. "What will it matter? We can carry only two humans at a time anyway."

"Two in your claws, at least four on your back," Shardas said.

"On our backs! Like common pack animals?!"

"If you cannot bring yourself to help them when they need you most," Velika said, "then you do not deserve their servitude, if you ever did." She turned to me. "Creel, help me with this harness. I can carry more than six, I am sure." She spoke in her own language, to make certain that they could all understand her.

"Yes, Your Majesty," I said promptly.

Together Luka and I got the harness undone, and settled the eggs there in the middle of the ring. Shardas and Velika at once took off to gather up some humans, with Vannyn and many others following them. Those left behind fidgeted awkwardly, and then began to fly out as well, one and two at a time, until only Darrym and Mannyl were left.

Darrym opened his mouth to say something cutting, but was interrupted by Feniul, who flew in with seven or eight humans clinging to his back in terror. Two more were in his claws, and looked only marginally more comfortable. He put them down outside the ring, and the rest climbed off his back with obvious relief.

"Creel! Luka! Are you well?"

"Yes, Feniul!" My heart skipped around in my chest. I had assumed my brother was safely away with our friends. But if Feniul was here . . . "Where's Hagen?"

"He's helping Leontes pack some alchemical something-or-others," Feniul said.

"Oh." My heartbeat returned to normal. Or almost—it was still a bit too fast and my throat was dry. "Have you seen Velika and Shardas?"

"Indeed. Niva and I were coming to look for you, when we realized that the volcano was erupting. We found Shardas and Velika in the forest, and they told us to gather humans and bring them here.

"Is this really the Great Temple of the First Mother?" He craned his neck around, looking at the carvings.

"Yes," I said, then made a little shooing gesture. "But hurry and bring more people, Feniul dear. There's no time for history lessons now."

"Oh, yes, yes!" He took off again, and almost collided with another dragon coming in.

It was Niva, draped with terrified humans. Luka and I helped them dismount, and she took off again. Soon there was a steady stream of dragons coming and going, leaving shaken and wide-eyed villagers in the temple they had always been forbidden to enter.

A few of the villagers dared to approach the ring, fascinated by the eggs within, but Luka and I stepped between them and the eggs, and they backed off. From their amazement, I understood that Velika's eggs were twice the size of any dragon eggs they had ever seen, and there were nearly twice as many in the clutch as had been laid within their memory. None of this surprised us, of course.

The dragon I had once served—Rannym—came in and dropped Ullalal and her daughters practically on top of me. He looked rather frantic now, and took off before their feet touched the ground. They were smoke-stained, and one of the daughters had a burn on her arm covered by a makeshift bandage.

More and more people were arriving with injuries, and many of them were weeping in a way that told me they had lost someone they loved to the fire or the lava. I started to pace around the eggs, itching to help but knowing there was nothing I could do. I had no experience with caring for burns, and some of the people were afraid of me.

Luka, who had what he called "field training," managed to convince a few people that he meant them no harm. While Ullalal washed burns, he bandaged them under her supervision.

And I paced around the eggs.

"Well, you're a lot of help, wearing a hole in the floor that way." Hagen came up behind me and gave me a rough slap on the back.

"Hagen!" I threw my arms around him and squeezed. "Where have you been?"

"Helping me," Leontes rumbled. "We have burn medicine here," he said loudly, in the dragon tongue.

At once Ullalal and several others went to him. Hagen pulled a basket from Leontes's back and began to hand out pots of something green and sticky.

After all of the pots but one had been distributed, Hagen took one and beckoned a couple of children over, smiling to put them at ease. They came, reluctantly, and showed him their burned fingers. Hagen began to rub the sticky stuff on them.

"When we saw the fires starting, Leontes and I did a quick run for some alo-alo plant he saw when we first arrived," he said cheerfully, as though he rubbed burn salve on strange, half-naked children every day. "We had to crush the plants in these pots before we could bring them—the salve has to set for an hour or so before you use it."

"I'm just glad that you're safe," I told him, and gave him another hug.

"Yes, yes." He patted my shoulder absently. "I wasn't worried about you," he went on, gesturing to another group of children. "After everything you've done in the last three years, I figured that a volcano would hardly catch your attention!"

I swatted him.

A Day and a Night and a Day

As the fires and lava flows continued, though, all laughter and jesting ceased. The last humans brought in were coughing from smoke inhalation or were burned so badly that I found it impossible to control my expression when I saw their wounds, and had to turn away for a moment.

After a time, even the dragons didn't dare to look for more survivors. For although their scales were impervious to the heat from forest fires, the lava could still burn them, and the smoke choke them as well.

Shardas and Velika, who had both suffered terrible burns in the First Dragon War, felt the heat from the volcano more keenly than the others. They said nothing, but I could see the stiffness in their movements. And I could see the memories in their eyes, of pain and darkness and fighting to stay alive. The memories were worse than the heat and the smoke, I felt sure.

Now that Velika was back with her eggs, I could help a little more with the people, though they still looked at me askance. To my surprise, it was Ullalal who made me feel the most welcome. She appeared grateful for the help, and respectful of my closeness with the king and queen.

Together, she and I organized what supplies there were,

distributed blankets, food, and water, and fetched Leontes when we found someone too badly injured for just a little salve to mend. With humans worth little more than chattel here, nothing approaching a human physician could be found, but Ullalal, with her knowledge of herbs, was the closest they had. She was not quite a physician, nor truly an alchemist.

"But she is willing to learn and has some knowledge of her own," Leontes said. "That will have to do."

Hagen helped, too, and one look at the vibrancy in his expression and movements made me realize that this, perhaps, was where my brother truly belonged.

During the long wait that followed, I took Leontes aside to tell him so.

"As the oldest living person in my family," I began, not sure how to phrase this. "Well, I do have an aunt and uncle, but they're not here. And also, well . . ."

"I am aware of the part your aunt played in your meeting Theoradus," Leontes said tactfully.

"Yes, indeed." I brushed futilely at my trousers, but they would have to be thrown away when this was over. If I ever got out of this temple. Off this continent. "I would like to offer my brother, Hagen, to you as an apprentice," I said finally.

"I am delighted to accept his services," Leontes said. "And I see no need for an apprentice fee, as there is nothing to purchase in the Far Isles." He chuckled. "But shall we say that he must serve under my tutelage for three years? At which time, I shall assess his knowledge and determine if he has mastered the arts sufficiently to set up his own laboratory."

"That sounds excellent." But I frowned. "We really

should compensate you," I said. "We shall have to have a cousin take care of Theoradus's museum, and also Hagen's orchards. Perhaps a percentage of the orchard's earnings, in the form of seeds or dry goods, could be brought to the Far Isles?"

"An excellent plan," said Leontes. "Ten percent of the orchard's earnings, for three years?"

"Very good." We bowed to each other and then he flew me down to the ring where we had set up camp.

Our camp was quite a strange sight: in the ring, which was the exact middle of the temple, the clutch of eggs was watched over by two enormous dragons. Around them were more dragons, huge and brightly colored, with Hagen, Luka, and me walking freely among them. In the far corners of the main floor, and throughout the temple, were the other dragons: small, dull colored, and with their eyes always upon Velika and her eggs. Their humans, some thousand people, huddled together by village. They did not address any dragon without being spoken to first; they did not make eye contact with a dragon at any time. It was heartbreaking to see how spiritless they were.

When Leontes and I arrived back at the ring to bring Hagen the news of his apprenticeship, the calls of congratulation from our dragon friends and the bashful way that Hagen hugged me and then Leontes caused a great many stares and so much muttering that it almost approached a roar.

"What is all this?" Mannyl had withdrawn into himself during the crisis, and had not spoken for more than a day. "What are you going on about?" The Elder One sniffed the air. "Tell me!"

"Leontes, who is an alchemist, has just agreed to take my brother, Hagen, as an apprentice," I said boldly, and Amacarin translated for me.

"A human, apprenticing to a dragon?" He spluttered incoherently for several minutes. "In *alchemy*?" The spluttering turned to coughs. "I will not have it! I will not have it!"

"But I will," Velika said firmly. "It is precisely what this world needs: humans and dragons working side by side. Not against each other, not keeping one another as slaves. Together."

"Never!" Mannyl's scream made me touch my ears to see if they were bleeding, and I saw that Luka had just done the same. "Never!"

But the screams took too much out of him, and he collapsed, panting, and said nothing more.

During the night Darrym began to keen, and we lit torches to see what the problem was.

The Elder One had passed away.

By the light of the pink torches, we all bowed our heads and sang the song of dragon mourning. I knew it all too well, although as a human I couldn't sing it properly, but I was surprised to find that all the local humans knew it, too. It seemed that mourning dragons was not forbidden to them. We stood, those of us who could, and sang until well after sunlight had trickled through the entrance. We rested briefly, and ate what little food there was, and then began again. A full dragon funeral would stretch for days, but these were only the songs that must be sung before a body was laid on its pyre.

And before that could be done, we would have to venture

outside the temple, Velika declared. We needed food, and it was time to see what was left in the aftermath of the eruption.

Once the second mourning song was done, Luka, Hagen, and I all rode on Shardas as he burst out into the dim sunlight and surveyed the scene below.

What had been spared by the volcano?

Very, very little.

Glassy Shore, Steaming Sea

It's like . . . like . . ." Words failed me, and I closed my mouth with a click of teeth. Perched on Shardas's back, I reached forward and put my arms around Luka, feeling my brother's hand on my shoulder from behind.

The forest was gone.

As far as we could see there was nothing but a vast ocean of steaming black rock. The mountains that rose out of the rocky plain were barren, their trees turned to ash. There was a river cutting through the plain, but its flow was sluggish and it was choked with ash and debris. Thick clouds of smoke still filled the sky, making it hard to breathe.

"It's all been destroyed," Luka said. "Their whole country."

"Yes," Shardas said gravely. "They will need to find a new home." He sighed heavily. "With us, I am sure."

"So you'll take them all to the Far Isles?" I found my voice at last. "The humans, too?"

"We have no other choice," he replied.

It was true. It would be murder to leave anyone, human or dragon, in this place. There was no food, no clean water, as far as I could see.

"Well, there're fish," Hagen pointed out. "I mean, for us

to eat right now," he amended as we all looked at him. "Of course you can't leave anyone here."

"I wonder how far the flow went into the ocean," Luka said. Looking north, we could see only more clouds.

"Let's find out," Shardas said.

He spread his wings and leaped into the air, gliding over the ripples and mounds of hardening lava. Here and there a streak of glowing orange showed where the molten rock still had not cooled completely.

While the endless fields of black rock that had once been forest were depressing, the shore was now rather breathtaking. Steam rose in clouds where the hot rock touched the water, but the sand of the shore had been fused into a glistening ribbon of greenish black glass.

Shardas hovered over it, poking with his claws and probing with his tail to see if he could land there.

"It's cool enough," he reported. "But too slick to provide any footing." He settled into the water instead, heaving a sigh as he did so. "Warm," he said, his eyes half-closed.

The steam was quite pleasant, though it made the hair that had escaped my braids stick to my face. It felt cleaner to breathe, certainly. Hagen slid down Shardas's back to his rump, and looked into the clear water as best he could.

"I think the fish might have been scared away," he reported.

"You are no doubt right," Shardas said. "Grab hold."

Hagen scrambled back to put his hands on my waist, I put mine on Luka's, and Luka gripped the ridge in front of him as tightly as he could. Shardas sank down until our boots were wet, then hit the bottom with all four feet and surged upward.

Streaming water, he skimmed the waves and circled around to the islet where we had first set up our camp. There was little there now: some spare ropes and baskets that had carried supplies, a fishing net or two laid out to dry. Shardas scooped one of these up in his foreclaws, and dragged it through the water a few times.

Nothing.

"The fish have either been frightened away, or were poisoned by the gases in the lava," he declared. "We're going to have to get far from here, soon, in order to find food."

We soared further over the ocean, to places where we had found fish before, and dragged the net through the water again and again. Not a single fish turned up, and we saw no sign of anything else—none of the strange, flat, diamond-shaped fish the Citatians called *rai'as*, no porpoises or even seabirds. We were the only living things for miles.

Gathering up the net, Shardas flew us back to the temple. Humans and dragons had gathered at the entrance, and some had even ventured down the side of the mountain. The elegant carvings were smoke-blackened, but otherwise undamaged, I was pleased to see.

What I was not pleased to see was Darrym, standing in the center of the entrance, roaring displeasure at Ullalal.

"She's not even his person," I hissed to Luka.

"Hush," Hagen said. "What is he saying?"

"None shall leave! None shall leave this place!" Darrym flamed into the air to make his point.

Some of the humans who had been climbing around the entrance started, and crept back inside the darkened temple. Amacarin, who was crouched on a ledge at the top of the entrance, leaped back and nearly lost his footing.

"I say, watch how you go there!"

Darrym's neck twisted, snakelike, as he looked up at Amacarin. "*You* are free to go at any time, of course," he said silkily. He turned his head and looked straight at Shardas. "Any of *you*. Any time."

"We will all be leaving soon," Shardas said, hovering just outside the entrance. "The lava traveled all the way to the ocean; there are no more fish, no plants or animals. You will need to come with us to the Far Isles, lest you starve."

A shout, to everyone's surprise, came from Ullalal.

She stood below Shardas, shaking her head vehemently. With a long finger she pointed to the south.

"No, there is nothing there," Darrym told her, but there was a strange edge to his voice.

Ullalal let loose with a string of words in her own language, all the while pointing to the south.

"Get back in the temple," Darrym snarled when she was through.

"Amacarin," Shardas said before Ullalal could respond, "take her south and see what the terrain is like there."

"At once." The blue-gray dragon dropped down from his perch and settled beside Ullalal. He extended one foreclaw to help her mount, and she stared at him. "You may ride on my back," he told her kindly.

Gingerly, she clambered over his shoulder and settled

just in front of his wings. He took off smoothly, keeping her balanced as best he could. Such solicitous behavior from Amacarin was still new to me, and I marveled afresh at the civilizing influence Gala had had on him.

But my attention was dragged away once again by Darrym. He was breathing like a blacksmith's bellows, and smoke came out of his nostrils. "You. Have. No. Right."

"I have every right," Shardas said, his voice like a blade.

"Not for long," Darrym said, and more smoke escaped from his mouth with the words.

"What is that?" Now Shardas's chest expanded, and we all gripped tight. Luka turned his face toward me, bracing for the wash of heat that would come if Shardas let loose his flame. "Do you threaten me?"

"No," Darrym said. "I *challenge* you."

Duel

Darrym has lost his mind," Hagen said with authority. "Shardas is twice his size, at the very least."

We were in the ring on the floor of the temple once more, telling Velika what was happening.

"And Shardas has already won a challenge against a much larger dragon," Luka added. "More than once, in fact."

I winced, thinking of those challenges. Shardas's own brother, Krashath, had objected to his kingship. In their first fight, long before my great-great-great-grandmother's time, Krashath had been wounded and presumed dead. When he returned, just last year, Shardas had defeated him once and for all.

That fight had been a horrible thing to see, and as much as I loathed Darrym, I wasn't looking forward to seeing it repeated. The smaller dragon was vastly outmatched: it would be a slaughter.

I fussed with the blanket that covered one of the eggs, waiting for Velika to speak up, to stop the fight. But she didn't. I finally looked at her, and saw that she was gazing at the carving on the wall just outside the ring.

"We knew we would have to fight," she said softly. "To

make our point, to get our eggs out of here. I just never thought it would be a duel, and not with someone we had once considered a friend."

"You don't really mean to let them do this?" I gave her a pleading look.

"Creel, we have no choice," Velika said. "We all wanted this to end without a conflict, and it will. It just won't end without bloodshed."

She had a point. And, moreover, if Shardas had to fight anyone, I preferred it to be Darrym over anyone else. He was a traitor, after all, and I could not believe that I, too, had once considered him a friend.

"Shardas! I am ready!"

We could see Darrym framed in the entrance of the temple. With the sun behind him, it was hard to make out his features, but he seemed to have grown several large spinal ridges quite suddenly.

"What are those?" Luka squinted at the dragon.

"Spears," Shardas said, his voice flat.

"Your spears?" My voice was a squeak.

"It appears that way," Shardas said quietly.

"I challenge you, Shardas," Darrym shouted again.

Murmurs and cries were coming now from the dragons within the temple, and the humans as well. They stared at Shardas, some fearful, some angry, but others with hope or approval. He nodded to them all.

"Darrym has challenged me," Shardas announced. "I go to face him. Let there be witnesses."

Every dragon in the temple scrambled about, gathering

up humans and then rushing to the entry. There was very nearly a collision, and Darrym had to dive out of the way before he was stampeded by his own people. Then Velika called two of our friends back.

"Leontes, Niva, guard the eggs," she ordered. "I will accompany my mate."

"And so will we," I said.

Taking Luka's hand, I mounted Velika without asking permission or waiting for an invitation. Hagen was right on our heels, and I thought about convincing him to stay behind, but if I was old enough to see such things, so was he, and I knew that it would be maddening to be trapped inside, listening and waiting for the outcome.

We were the last ones out of the temple, and Darrym was waiting. He stood in a large ring formed by the dragons on a relatively flat area of cooled lava. In his foreclaws he held the spears that Shardas had made so long ago. Or so it seemed, after all we had been through.

"You have the advantage of size," Darrym said. "I thought I would even things out."

"If you must," Shardas said calmly.

Vannyn came forward. "Darrym, I beg of you, do not do this."

"You cannot stop a challenge for the kingship," Darrym screeched.

"But remember," Velika said coldly, before Vannyn could answer, "remember that the queen must also accept the winner. And I find it hard to imagine a scenario where I would accept *you*." Then she leaned closer, and almost whispered to

Darrym, though still loudly enough for most of the gathered dragons to hear. "And if you kill the father of my children before they are even hatched, *I promise you will pay.*" She sat back, and we scrambled to arrange ourselves on her shoulders where we could see everything.

Vannyn looked about to object again, but Shardas caught his eye. The gold dragon shook his head emphatically.

"It was his decision," Shardas said. "The challenge has been set, and he must fight or die."

"I will win!"

Letting out a roar, Darrym lifted one of the spears and threw it at Shardas's breast.

Shardas lunged to the side, and then batted at the spear with his tail before it could strike the watchers behind him. He picked it up in his own foreclaws, and moved aside again as Darrym threw another. This one nearly got Shardas's head, but he ducked just in time. It clattered against the ridges of his spine and slid down his back. I saw that where it had struck it had pierced between two scales, but Shardas appeared not to notice and there was only the faintest streak of blood.

Now Shardas, tired of waiting for Darrym to throw his own spears against him, leaped into action. Holding the spear he had captured in one foreclaw, he attacked Darrym, stabbing at the other dragon and lashing him with his tail. He shot a jet of flame at Darrym, and all the watchers sensibly moved back several more dragon-lengths.

Darrym countered with his own fire, and with another spear that went wide as Shardas used his wings to carry himself to one side. Then Shardas moved forward in a rush, flaming as he went, and the fire caught Darrym's face and neck along one side.

Screaming with rage and now blinded in one eye, Darrym still had a spear in each foreclaw, which he used to stab wildly at Shardas. A lucky hit caught in the thick plates that covered Shardas's breast, and the dragon king gave a roar of pain. He tried to pull the spear free but it snapped off near one end, and the sharp point was still stuck fast in his chest as Shardas hurled the rest of the glass spear back at Darrym, hitting him hard just behind one shoulder. Where the scales hinged there, the spear sank deep, and Darrym fell.

"Do you submit to me?" Shardas's breathing was ragged, but his voice was calm.

"Never," Darrym hissed, and he threw his last spear.

Shardas deflected it easily, and then cast aside his own remaining weapon. I gave a little gasp, but Vannyn sent me a reassuring look. Shardas was moving close to Darrym, one foreclaw held up with the claws fully extended. There was something ritualistic in his movements, and I realized that this was likely the final blow, the one that would end Darrym's life.

Then suddenly Darrym's tail swept around, knocking Shardas off his feet. His wings extended as he tried to regain his balance, which gave Darrym the time he needed to get up again. He flew into the air, listing drunkenly to one side because of his wounded shoulder, and flamed at Shardas as he went.

The fire caught the gold dragon's wings, which had been so badly burned two years ago, and Shardas screamed in pain.

But he followed Darrym into the air, and they began to fight as dragons have since the beginning of the world: with four sets of claws, with tails and fire and teeth, spinning and tumbling through the air.

I could barely stand to watch, but forced myself to, knowing that I couldn't truly bear to miss a single blow. It didn't take long for the duel to end, though. Both dragons were injured, but Shardas had the advantage of years and experience, besides the more obvious superiority of size.

As Shardas's golden claws raked Darrym's throat, the small, brown dragon gave one last gurgling scream. He fell to the lava field with a thud, narrowly missing a group of humans who had scrambled out of the way at the last minute. Shardas soared down afterward, landing beside us.

He had several rents in his wings, a burn or two, and the point of a glass spear in his breast, but seemed steady enough on his feet. He looked around at the assembled dragons and humans gravely.

"Would anyone else care to challenge me?"

Mutters and head shakes.

"Would anyone else care to cast doubt upon the lineage of their queen?"

Mutters and head shakes, and even some loud declarations of "No!" and "Hail our queen!"

"We will prepare to move to the Far Isles tomorrow," Shardas said. He spread his gold wings with a snap, and flew back into the temple.

"Now hold still," I said to Shardas after he had gotten settled beside his eggs and his queen, and Niva and Leontes had been told what had happened. "And try not to burn me to ash, please."

"What do you mean?"

Without answering, I put one foot on Shardas's chest; Luka put his hands on my hips to brace me, and I grabbed hold of the end of the spear that stuck out of his breastplate. With a yank I pulled it free, and Shardas let out a roar that shook some rock dust down from the upper ledges.

"That will teach you to engage in duels like a hatchling." Velika sniffed as Leontes rushed to pack an herb-infused moss into the wound.

"I suppose it will," Shardas said between gritted teeth.

Where There Is Green

But we could not leave without Amacarin, and he and Ullalal were investigating the south until late the next day. When they returned I saw that they had good news, for Ullalal's eyes were sparkling and Amacarin looked very pleased with himself.

"There is a ravine, a rift that divides this continent," he reported. "The lava did not cross it, nor did the fire."

"And the other side is green?" Velika looked up from busily packing her eggs back in the net. She caught me fingering the silk that bound one of the joins, and gave me a sympathetic look.

"Greener than the forest before the eruption," he confirmed. "And there are people there. People who do not belong to any dragons."

"Runaways," came the disdainful reply of my former master Rannym from where he stood near Mannyl's husk. "Those who refused to serve us."

"You mean, those who were too smart to let themselves be enslaved by you," I snapped, not caring that he couldn't understand me. Then I blushed, for I had come to think very highly of Ullalal.

"But," Luka said, raising a cautionary hand, "what if these people don't want to accept a flood of immigrants?" As a prince he knew a great deal about such matters.

"On the contrary," Amacarin said. "That is what delayed us. First we had to make them understand that I was not there to enslave them." He huffed at the very idea. "Then we asked if there was room for more humans in their lands." He preened. "It was difficult: they do not speak our language, but I recognized their tongue as a form of Tonlulat and was eventually able to make myself understood. Once we got over that difficulty, they were quite willing to accept the refugees."

"Tonlulat?" Luka looked mystified, and I was secretly glad that for once I wasn't the only one whose knowledge was lacking.

"There is some delightful poetry in that language," Amacarin said. "I have a fine collection of it. I had no idea it originated in such a place."

"Tonlulat." Smiling, Ullalal turned the word over in her mouth, her voice soft and almost musical.

"Yes," Amacarin told her, head bobbing, before he turned back to Velika. "Once I recognized it, I began to understand this woman better as well. I think they are Tonlulan, or used to be."

"Then you should stay here, with your own people," Velika said to Ullalal. She raised her head, and announced to the temple at large: "The humans of this land should stay, and learn to live as they once did, free of dragon servitude."

Immediately several dragons began to protest. I suspected they had meekly agreed to travel to the Far Isles only because they would still have their villages with them, and hoped to reestablish themselves as masters over the humans in some out-of-the-way place where Velika and Shardas would not notice.

It was interesting to see, as well, that no humans protested this. Many of them looked nervous, but mostly they seemed excited, whispering among themselves and hugging their children, as though already imagining their young ones growing up free.

"For this reason," Shardas said, indicating the protests, "we will not take any humans with us to the Far Isles." I jabbed him with my elbow. "Saving those three who came with us," he amended. "If you are to put aside this abominable slavery of the humans, then you must have all temptation removed."

"I agree with my consort," Velika announced. "The Tonlulan people should feel free to remain here, in their ancestral lands. After the funeral for your elder, we shall take the humans south."

"Tomorrow," Amacarin said to Ullalal and her daughters, "you will have a new home."

She patted him on the foreleg in a way that was both bold and fond. Luka and I shared a look, and then laughed at the expression of surprise on Shardas's face.

It was Velika who voiced my thoughts: "Having a mate has been most improving for Amacarin."

The Lost Ones

Not knowing what to expect, we landed to the south of the village that Amacarin and Ullalal had found the day before. Well, Amacarin called it a village, but really it was the same size as Carlieff Town, if not larger. Few of the buildings were taller than two stories, but they were of stone with clay-tile roofs, and the streets were paved with flat, black rocks that were undoubtedly of a volcanic origin.

We startled some strange, long-necked, shaggy creatures that had been grazing in the field, and I swear that one of them spit at Feniul. Hagen slipped off Leontes's neck and started to follow the creatures into the little copse of trees they had taken shelter in, fascinated, but I called him back.

"They spit," I said. "They probably bite as well."

"They are ill-tempered things," Amacarin agreed. "But I saw someone riding one yesterday. It did not look like a smooth-gaited beast, though."

Now there was even more longing in Hagen's face.

Luka started laughing. "I shall buy you one when you finish your apprenticeship," he told my brother. "It can be your mastery-gift. A hairy, spitting cow-horse."

"*Unayama*," Ullalal's oldest daughter said to me. She pointed at the things. "*Unayama*."

Vannyn nodded. "Yes, I believe that is what they are called. They are very tough meat, so our ancestors got rid of the ones living on our side of the country. A shame, really. They have such soft fur."

Our attention was caught by a large group of people streaming out of the town toward us. At their head was a sort of open carriage, draped with fur rugs, and pulled by two proud *unayamas*. More people followed, some on foot, some riding *unayamas*. The people wore brightly colored cloths draped about their hips and sometimes over their chests, but their main covering seemed to be jewelry. Their necklaces were fine, though: gold beads, and red and blue and purple stones. They were a splendid people, rich and proud, and I worried anew for Ullalal and her friends.

But I needn't have.

When they reached the pasture, the townspeople began to run. With outstretched arms festooned with bracelets, they embraced any human they came upon. There were many tears, and they cried out in a loud singsong, the same words over and over.

At a nudge from Shardas, Amacarin translated.

"They are welcoming the 'lost ones,'" he said, clearly also surprised by the warmth of this welcome. Now many of the townspeople were taking off their own jewelry and putting it on the people with us. I was relieved to see that the dragon-people, as I had come to think of them, also seemed moved, and they handed back their own lesser adornments with tears and kisses.

At last the woman who had ridden in the back of the carriage came forward. She had necklaces so thick across her chest that I wondered how she could stand straight, and there were feathers braided in her graying hair. She called out in an imperious voice, and Amacarin answered, which made her frown. All of the townspeople were studiously ignoring the dragons, and it clearly displeased her to speak to one.

Ullalal also came forward, and with Amacarin's help spoke to the woman, most certainly the ruler of this place. It was some time before Amacarin had a chance to translate for our benefit, but when he did the gist of it was this:

The magnificent woman was indeed their queen for, like dragons, they were a people ruled by their queens. This was not the largest of her cities, but she had traveled all night so that she might be there to welcome back the lost ones when they arrived. Her people had mourned those enslaved by the dragons for many generations, but knew they had no way to defeat their cousins' captors. It pleased them greatly to see the dragon-people freed, and they would find homes for all of them. In return they asked that no dragon ever again cross the ravine that divided the land.

Velika, through Amacarin, explained that the volcano had destroyed the lands of the dragons, and that she was now taking them away. She promised, one queen to another, that dragons would not again trouble the humans of this land, and this seemed to satisfy the feather-bedecked ruler.

Evening was coming, and we had barely eaten in days. Amid cries of excitement in their singsong language, the people brought tables and a feast was spread before us. Sides of beef and fruits and vegetables in huge bushel baskets were provided for the dragons, and there was music and dancing.

Luka and I joined the dancing, though we didn't know the steps. I nearly knocked over a small woman wearing nothing but a red skirt and a necklace of gold beads. She smiled good-naturedly, and soon Luka was dancing with her and I was dancing with a man who was either her husband or her brother.

As dawn touched the tops of the mountains, furs were laid out and we settled down to sleep, not waking until it was nearly noon and the sun could not be ignored any longer. More food was being brought from the town, and Shardas ordered us to eat quickly; he wanted to leave as soon as we were satisfied.

It was time for the dragons to return home.

There were some tears from humans who had been fond of their dragon-masters. I noticed that Ullalal shed none, but her youngest daughter was caught trying to climb into a basket slung over Rannym's shoulder. In the end the girl was hauled off, weeping, by her sisters. Ullalal herself came forward and thanked Shardas and Velika, bid a fond farewell to Amacarin, and then came to me.

"Thank you," she said through Amacarin. She gave me a necklace of bone beads and then rejoined her daughters.

Finally Velika took to the air and coolly said that any dragon who did not follow her immediately would be punished.

She turned and flew north without looking back. Niva, Leontes, Roginet, Amacarin, Feniul, and Shardas all waited to make sure that the queen's orders were followed. At last they, too, took to the air, with Luka and me aboard Shardas and Hagen on Leontes, and headed over the ravine and across the fields of cooling lava, toward the distant Far Isles.

Home

The reception for the lost ones had been warm, but it was nothing compared to what occurred when we at last reached the Far Isles.

Those dragons who had been left behind were flying patrol, watching for us, and when we arrived there was much roaring and flaming, with one of the sentries streaking back to the shore to take the news to the others. Mates, hatchlings, and friends rushed to meet us.

Gala crashed right into Amacarin, bringing him down into the surf with her in a most undignified tangle. Ria, Feniul's mate, twined her neck with his in midair, and they landed clumsily on the sand beside their children, who were screaming with shrill delight and doing their best to flame a greeting for their father.

Seeing the net of eggs slung beneath her, an honor guard formed about Velika, guiding her back to the portion of the shore that was her and Shardas's special place. Solicitous females helped Velika out of the harness and nestled the eggs into the sand. They wanted to take them immediately back to Velika and Shardas's cave, but both of the royal pair objected.

"Let them rest in the sun," Velika said. "They have been kept below the earth too much." She shuddered.

"Who are these strangers?" Gala had released Amacarin, who was now being swarmed by more dragonlets than I could count.

She was staring, as were many of the dragons who had remained on the Far Isles, at the newcomers with us. Brown and green, small, and looking by turns shy or mutinous, they were landing in the water just offshore, uncertain of whether they would be welcomed.

"These are our kin who were lost to us for many years," Velika said.

I had to admire her regal bearing: after days of flight, after all that she had been through, she sat on the sands like the queen she was and reshaped her people's lives with a few sentences.

"Their lives have, until now, been vastly different from ours, and we must assist them in learning to enjoy our ways," she continued. "They will need shelter, and friendship—but I suppose that will come in time."

Vannyn came forward. "We are most grateful for all that you offer us, Queen Azure-Wing," he said. "We shall endeavor not to be a burden to you, or to our newfound kin."

Luka and I were still perched on Shardas's back, too tired and too tense to dismount. Now that the speeches were done, the dragon midwives were gathering around Velika's eggs once more.

"Are they all right?" I slid down from Shardas's back, and

found myself swaying until I nearly pitched forward onto my knees.

I felt as though the ash from the volcano would never completely leave my lungs. I was filthy and my clothing was worn to shreds. Riding a dragon was not relaxing: my thighs were stiff from holding on and my hands had been scraped by the edges of more scales and horns than I cared to remember.

"Are they all right?" I repeated the question.

Luka staggered over to me and helped me sit in the sand beside the eggs. Hagen soon joined us, lying down beside the sandy nest with one arm over his eyes.

The midwives tutted, and asked questions about when the eggs had been clutched, and how long they had been carried in a harness. They even knocked on them gently, as though asking if the hatchlings were at home. I started to laugh, weakly, but was brought up short by the sound of knocking from *inside* the eggs.

It seemed that the hatchlings *were* at home, and eager to come out. The midwives clucked in satisfaction, and assured the nervous parents that their dear little ones appeared to be none the worse for their travails.

For the first time since Velika's abduction, the tension in Shardas's shoulders seemed to unknot, and he collapsed in the sand beside his children's eggs. Velika lay beside him and nodded at me in a meaningful way.

Groaning, I lurched to my feet and took charge.

"Thank you, thank you all," I said loudly. "The king and queen need their rest now. If you will join Prince Luka and me farther down the beach, I'm sure a celebratory feast is in order.

The royal family, however, will be dining here. Alone." I pointed to a half-grown dragon hovering nearby: Gala's daughter, Riss. "It's your duty to wait upon them tonight. There will be no questions, no pestering. Bring them food, and then leave. The rest of us will be happy to tell you all that has happened." I flapped my hands. "Now. Shoo!"

"Masterful dragon herding," Luka said out of the corner of his mouth as we walked down the beach.

We both stopped to take our shoes off, and I resolved to have someone bring me a large tub and some fresh water so that I could have a proper bath. Just as soon as I ate. And ate. And maybe slept first . . .

"What can I say? It's a gift," I replied absently.

I was staring down the beach at the wide expanse of white sand where the dragons had congregated. Someone was building a bonfire; someone else was lighting tall torches set in the sand, for the sun was sinking now. Food was brought, and Ria guided us humans over to a crude log bench and urged us to sit.

"Creel, I can see your brain working," Hagen said. "What are you plotting now?"

"She is going to overthrow the Triunity," Luka joked, and then sobered when he saw my brother's expression of horror. "Not truly, though. Right, Creel?"

"Of course not!" I flapped a hand at him. "It's just that I was thinking, with the exception of Marta and Tobin and Alle, and Miles and Isla, everyone I really care about is here on this island. But in a few days we'll be leaving, to go back to the King's Seat and get married in front of . . ." I hesitated, and then plowed on. "Well, in front of a bunch of near strangers and relations who normally don't give two pennies about me!" To my surprise, I started to cry. "Shardas and Velika aren't even welcome in Feravel, let alone in a chapel. How can I get married in a place that doesn't welcome my friends? No, not friends: they're my family!"

Luka and Hagen both put their arms around me, awkwardly. Embarrassed, I shook them off, but gently, and busied myself with wiping my face on a filthy sleeve.

"When I proposed, you said you would need to be married outdoors," Luka said slowly. "Because the head of your family was a dragon. I confess I was startled when you agreed to a chapel wedding so easily."

"I've never heard of anyone getting married outdoors, unless they were Moralienin," I said. "It's just not done."

"Dear, dear sister," Hagen said with mock sagacity, "after all your boasting that you have set every new fashion in the King's Seat for the past three years"—I punched his shoulder and he winced but carried on—"you mean to tell me that you can't start a new fashion for outdoor weddings, too?"

I made as if to punch him again, but didn't. I was staring down the sand again, at the bonfire, and the torches.

"I don't know if it will become the fashion," I said softly, taking Luka's hand. "But we're getting married right here," I continued, in my most no-nonsense tone. "I'm not leaving the Far Isles until we're married."

"Done!" Luka kissed me.

"Well, that shuts out our beloved aunt and equally light-minded cousins," Hagen said. "They'll never agree to ride a dragon." He let out a sigh of deep satisfaction as a young dragon brought us a platter of roasted meats and grilled fruit to share. "I might actually enjoy this wedding after all. Caxon knows, the food will be good."

Unexpected Guests

Creel! Creel! I knew it! I knew you would get married here! It's *gorgeous!*"

Marta ran down the beach toward me, waving her hands in the air with glee. She was wearing a pink tunic and trousers and wide ivory colored sash that I strongly suspected she had stolen from my wardrobe.

We hugged fiercely until Tobin came up, and then there was more hugging and the boys tried to outdo each other with backslaps. We were joined by Ria and her children, and there were introductions, interrupted by a high-pitched yapping followed by earsplitting shrieks.

"Pippin!" Marta knelt down to gather up the little white ball of hair that had been the lapdog of Princess Amalia of Roulain and now ruled Feniul's kennel.

Despite her size, Pippin was an alpha female, though I hadn't seen much of her since I'd come to the Far Isles. Now I understood why: trailing through the sand behind her were three minuscule brown and white puppies. Bringing up the rear was their father, a brown dog at least twice Pippin's size. We admired her puppies until the shrieking couldn't be avoided.

"Hello, Ruli," Marta said finally. The monkey she had bought in Citatie was swinging from Ria's horns and screaming at us. I'd run afoul of the little beast a number of times in the past weeks, and quickly fished a couple of nuts from a purse at my waist. I handed them to Marta, who threw them at her erstwhile pet to make him be quiet.

When he had taken the treats and scampered away, Marta brushed her hands together.

"Now then!" She started walking up the beach. "Are the guesthouses this way? I want to wash, and then we need to get to work. If you want to be married next week, when both moons are full, we've got a lot to do."

Avoiding her eyes, I said, "I don't know what you mean— I've been working on my dress for months."

"You're a terrible liar, Creel. You always have been," Marta said briskly. "I knew the minute we finished talking through the speaking pool that something was wrong. You very obviously didn't mention your wedding gown, even though it's all you've talked about for six months. It got dirty, didn't it? Or you lost a part?"

She realized that no one was following her, and turned around. Seeing the look on my face, and Luka's face, her mouth opened into an "O."

"*How bad is it?*"

"It's not really a gown anymore, so much as a large pile of ribbons," Luka said as tactfully as he could.

I covered my face with my hands.

"Creel! Caxon's bones! What did you do?"

"I saved a clutch of dragon eggs," I said, lowering my

hands from my red face. "And I'm not going to tell the whole story until Alle gets here, because I don't want to relive it over and over again."

Marta shook her head at me, then squinted into the distance. "Well, I can see two more dragons coming right now," she said. "So it shouldn't be long. Feniul had some sort of bet going with Leontes, which is how we got here first. I thought my hair was going to be blown right off my head."

The others did arrive quickly: Alle, Tobin's sister, Ulfrid, Luka's brother, Miles, and his wife, Isla. To avoid causing an uproar, we had invited only these few chosen friends, contacting Marta through a speaking pool and sending her to tell the rest. King Caxel had no idea that his younger son was about to be married in this unorthodox fashion, and we figured it was better this way.

But then Leontes smiled at us and pointed with a wing in the direction they had come. "My mate is bringing the other guests," he said. "They should be here shortly."

"Other guests?" I frowned. "Who?"

"You'll see."

Marta and Alle winked at each other, and Miles was smiling broadly. When Niva landed, we saw why.

I had a horrified flash of my aunt arriving with all my cousins, to complain about the sand and the heat and all the dragons, and sweat broke out on my upper lip. But if it were Aunt Reena, surely Miles wouldn't be smiling?

To my delight, the Duke and Duchess of Mordrel clambered down from Niva's back and rushed to embrace us. I greeted them with real pleasure. The duchess made much of my embroidered tunic and trousers, and that reminded me of my wedding gown dilemma again.

Marta and Alle, standing nearby, heard her, and I could see that they had been reminded as well. They immediately came to my side.

"We have a lot to do," Marta said briskly. "If someone can show us where we will be staying, and we can get our luggage unpacked, we'll need to get to work."

"Yes, please, everyone come this way." Gala stood at the head of the path that led to the guesthouses. "We have houses prepared, although some of you may have to share now." Shardas and Velika had designated her the hostess for the wedding, and she was doing an admirable job.

She led us down the shady path to the guesthouses. The Mordrels would have their own and Tobin and Marta easily agreed to share with Ulfrid. I told Alle to put her things with mine. Luka was already sharing with Hagen, so the most crowded house would have been his, now that his brother and sister-in-law had arrived. But Hagen solved the problem, saying he would move his things into Leontes and Niva's cave.

At least until the wedding.

Shardas had told me that he and Feniul were preparing a special house for Luka and me, but we were not to see it until after the ceremony. Which was all right with me, since just thinking about it made me blush furiously.

I was helping Alle shake out her gowns and hang them on the hooks on the wall next to mine when Marta whipped into the house with a twinkle in her eyes, a basket on one arm, and Pippin and her family at her heels. Marta plopped the basket down on the bed, then boosted the tiny dogs up as well. They sat neatly in a row and watched with their dark eyes, heads cocked in identical poses of curiosity.

Wanting to avoid what was coming next, I rubbed the little puppies behind their ears until Alle cleared her throat loudly and Marta started tapping her foot with a sharp sound on the wooden floor. I turned around to explain what had happened in the forest far to the south, and instead saw . . . a wedding gown.

"I don't believe it!" While they grinned with pride, I put both hands to my cheeks, and felt tears start in my eyes.

It was Marta's wedding gown—I could tell by the skirt, which I myself had painstakingly embroidered with clusters of flowers and tiny crystals. But Marta and Alle had taken off the high ruff to lower the neckline the way I preferred, and slashed the sleeves to put in lace inserts. Only someone who had seen Marta's gown every day for months, as I had, would recognize it, but even if they did it wouldn't matter.

It was gorgeous.

Eggshells

The weeks I had spent down in the lesser temple waiting for the eggs to harden had seemed eternal, but the one leading to my wedding went by in the blink of an eye.

We had to do the final fitting for Marta's attendant gown, since she insisted that only my stitching made her waist appear small enough. She and Alle had matching gowns of pale blue, embroidered with dragon scales and flowers in shades of turquoise and silvery gray. We had planned them before I decided to be married in the Far Isles, and I couldn't be more pleased at the way the clear waters that surrounded the island complemented the gowns.

Ria and Gala were putting their heads together with Isla and the duchess over the decorations, so after the attendants' gowns were finished, Marta and Alle and I only had to worry about fitting my gown. I put it off until the day before the wedding, however, convinced that something terrible would happen if I touched it: a stain, a snag, *something*.

So it was with great trepidation that I tried the gown on at last. I took a bath, made Marta and Alle wash their hands, and even swept the floor of my house first. My friends helped me into it, and I kept my eyes closed as they laced the tiny, tiny ribbons that ran up the back.

"Open your eyes, Creel," Marta said in a breathy voice.

I dared to look at last.

It fit like a dream: bodice tight, skirt flaring to just the right length. Marta and I were similar in size, and of course we kept straw-stuffed dummies made to our sizes in the shop. The sleeves were the right length too, just fitted enough without impeding movement. I sighed, and grinned, and twisted to look at myself from the back.

"Perfect," Alle agreed. "Perfect."

"It's better than the one I had—" I was cut off in mid-sentence by the sound of roaring.

Many dragons roaring. In a high, strange way I had never heard before.

We ran out of the guesthouse and down the path, nearly colliding with Miles and the Duke of Mordrel as they came out of Luka's house. We all raced for the beach and my only concession to my delicate, white skirts was holding them high off the sands. I was fleetingly grateful that I was barefoot, and didn't need to worry about ruining my new satin slippers.

All the dragons were streaming down the shore toward Shardas and Velika's private section of beach. They had their mouths open wide and were roaring or trilling—it was a bizarre combination of both.

"What is it? What's happening?"

Some were flying, but Feniul and Ria ran out of the jungle and started trotting up the beach beside us. They were streaming a trail of children like a parade.

"The hatching!" Feniul stopped roaring long enough to say the words with an explosion of joy. "The hatching!"

Luka caught up with us, and I told him the news as we ran. He linked his arm through mine and helped me speed along the sands. My heart was pounding against my tight bodice. We would see Shardas and Velika's eggs hatch!

Perhaps.

When we got to their section of the beach, there was such a solid wall of dragon bodies that I couldn't see anything but scales in front of me. Some of the dragons hovered in the air so that they could get a better look. Then Velika raised her head high (I could just catch a glimpse of the end of her snout), and said, "Where is Creelisel?"

"Here!" I jumped up and down.

"Make way for her, please."

Reluctantly, the dragons began to clear a path.

"Make way for all the humans," Shardas said.

We gathered in a ring around the sandy nest. The eggs were glowing red, and rocking slightly. I reached out to touch one, then drew back, but Velika nodded at me and I touched the nearest egg. It was so hot that I quickly pulled back again, and smiled at the queen dragon with a welling of emotion in my breast too great to express.

"We wish to have all our friends with us," Shardas announced loudly. "Human and dragon. One of these eggs will produce the future queen of the dragons, and there must be witnesses. For the first time in history, some of those witnesses will be human, to build stronger bonds between all our people—dragon and human."

We were all solemn, but then one of the eggs rocked itself up on end and we gasped. I fell to my knees beside the egg, fists clenched, and began *willing* it to hatch a female. Leontes had told us that if the first egg to hatch was a female—the future queen—it was a very good omen.

Suddenly cracks appeared in the shell. They grew longer and wider, and with a final snapping sound, a baby dragon the size of a large dog tumbled out.

Its wings were wet, its scales looked like crumpled paper, its eyes weren't open, and it was covered in goo. It was hideous and sweet all at the same time. It opened its mouth and mewed, and the dragons roared with joy.

"The future queen, the future queen," one of them bellowed in my ear.

Another egg was hatching now, but I was busy kissing Luka in celebration.

And then the sound of the roaring changed.

Alle screamed, and I whirled around just in time to see a gray dragon—Rannym, the very dragon I had once served as a *klgaosh*—scoop up the tiny queenlet and leap into the sky with her.

It was desperation, or madness, for he was surrounded by dragons loyal to Shardas and Velika. But still he pumped his wings, heading up and up. Shardas bellowed and leaped into the air after him, but it was Luka who moved the fastest.

He had been hunting small jungle deer with Tobin for our wedding feast. He still wore his bow and quiver, and before Shardas's wings could fully extend, Luka had nocked an arrow and aimed directly at the eye of the gray dragon.

Rannym screamed and dropped the tiny, mewling hatchling.

Shardas snatched at his firstborn daughter, but she was so wet she slid out of his claws.

I didn't even think.

I grabbed Tobin's shoulders and we ran forward, locking our arms in a loose cradle. The hatchling fell into our arms with a plop. My knees buckled and Tobin knelt quickly so that we didn't drop her. She keened and pressed herself against my chest, and I felt tears dripping down my cheeks onto her.

"You're all right, it's all right, precious baby," I murmured over and over.

The arrow had dealt a mortal wound to my old master, but the others didn't even let his body fall to the sands. He was plucked from the air and taken far out over the sea, to be dropped with a splash we could see from the shore.

Tobin and I carried the future queen to her parents, who were huddled over their remaining eggs. More of them were cracking now, and Velika looked wild, not certain who to comfort first. We placed the firstborn in her foreclaws, and she settled down.

"Creel," Shardas said, and his voice was choked with emotion, "Creel . . ."

"It's a good thing you saved me from those bandits all those years ago," I told him.

Then, just as I had when Shardas had first saved me, I fainted.

I woke up on the sand, in Luka's arms, surrounded by cheeping baby dragons and a distraught Marta.

"The gown is *ruined*," she wailed.

Defying the Curse Again

"Creel? What are you doing in there?" Luka knocked urgently on the door of my little house.

"I'm fine," I said. "I just have to fix this."

"Marta says there's no way to fix it," he replied. Even muffled by the door, his voice was gentle. "I'm sorry. She said you were acting rather strange about it." He cleared his throat. "If you need to delay the wedding . . ."

"The moons will be full tomorrow night," I reminded him. "A member of the royal family can only get married when both moons are full. We'd have to wait another two months."

"We can wait," he said stoutly.

"Luka, my darling, go away and let me fix this so that we won't have to," I said. "And tell Marta to stop coming around weeping and wringing her hands: I'll be fine."

"You're sure?"

"Quite, quite sure."

Even his sigh was audible through the door. "Very well. I shall see you in the morning?"

"At the wedding," I promised.

I waited until his steps crunched down the path. I had

a lot of work to do, and didn't want any more distractions. Arrayed on dressmakers' dummies in front of me were not one or two, but three gowns.

Or at least the remnants of them.

There was Marta's remade gown, covered with pinkish baby dragon goo that had dried nasty and stiff. There was the bodice of my original wedding gown. The skirts had been ruined, but the bodice had survived with only a little crumpling of the heavy silk.

And there was the gold gown.

Quite possibly the finest gown I had ever made, finer even than my wedding gown, it was reworked from a castoff of Princess Amalia's, the gold velvet and satin almost entirely covered with my richest embroidery. On the heavy overskirts were images of stained glass windows telling the story of the Maiden Irial and her beloved dragon companion, Zalthus. On the bodice and down the sleeves there was red and blue and green embroidery in abstract patterns. In its last incarnation, for Miles and Isla's wedding, I had replaced the gold satin underskirts with blue silk, the memory of which had given me an idea. And the bodice, really, for all its fine work, was nothing when compared with the glory of the skirts. The gold gown had been a gift for Gala in order to rid myself of the apparently cursed garment, but when I told her of my dire need she had graciously handed it back. I promised her that I would return it after the wedding, although it might be altered somewhat.

Somewhat.

Brides married before the Triunity in Feravel were

supposed to wear white from the skin out. But we weren't in Feravel, and I was being married before a thousand or more dragons.

Their hushed voices were not reassuring.

Alle had covered the mirror while she and Marta got me dressed and did my hair, and now I took a deliberate step toward it. The wedding would start any minute, and I had to see.

"No, let me," Marta said softly. She whipped aside the long shawl that obscured the glass.

Rice powder had been brushed on my face, lightly, to make my freckles less prominent, and coral paint applied to my lips. My hair was braided with strands of creamy white pearls (a gift from Isla) and wrapped around my head like a crown. Around my throat was a white satin ribbon with a golden dragon brooch (a gift from Luka) pinned to it.

The bodice of my original wedding gown was silk, embroidered with shimmering white threads in patterns that looked abstract at first glance. Close up, though, they were the entwined figures of dragons. It had a stiffened collar, about half a hand wide, to frame my neck, and was cut daringly low. The sleeves were tight to the elbow and then flared over my fore-arms. They stopped short of the wrist, to show off the pearl bracelets that had been Miles's gift.

I had sewn the gold overskirt to the white bodice. It was split, front and back, and beneath it I had sewn in the white silk underskirts from Marta's gown. Hagen had bored a small hole in the lumpy glass flower Shardas had made for me, and

I had sewn it to the waist of the gown, right where the gold overskirts split. The gold velvet, with its rainbow of embroidery, stood out starkly against the white silk of the rest of the gown.

Even I had to admit: I looked magnificent.

"No bride in Feravel has ever looked as marvelous, or ever will again," Marta said in a hushed voice. "And other than the dragons there are only a dozen people to see it!" Her voice rose to a wail at this.

Alle and I just laughed at her, and then it was time to begin. Miles came to fetch us, and I watched his expression as Marta opened the door to reveal me in all my glory. He was dumbstruck, and then a grin took over his face.

"So beautiful!" He kissed me carefully on the cheek. "Are you ready?"

"I suppose I am," I said.

Luka and Tobin met us at the foot of the path. Their eyes widened when they saw me, and Luka whistled. Luka and I kissed as he took my arm. We waited there together, breathing nervously, while our friends and family preceded us down the beach to the place marked for the ceremony. I couldn't really see anything: there were so many dragons gathered there. But they had left an aisle for us, and a rich, narrow carpet had been laid over the sand so that we wouldn't stumble.

There were no musicians, but the dragons hummed low. Clutching each other's hands tightly, Luka and I made our way down the long, carpeted aisle between rows of staring dragons. At the front of the gathering were the humans: Hagen and the Mordrels, Miles and Isla, Tobin and Ulfrid. Marta and Alle were to stand ready behind me, to fan me if I became faint and to pass me Luka's rings when the time came.

Just behind them were Shardas and Velika, using their tails to confine their day-old children. Shardas lowered his muzzle, and I stroked it with the hand that wasn't clutching Luka's.

As an alchemist, Leontes had the authority to marry us as long as we registered the marriage with a priest of the Tri-unity within the next six months. We simply wouldn't tell anyone that this particular alchemist was a dragon. Leontes cleared his throat, and I turned to face him.

And saw the altar he stood beside.

It was a three-tiered Triune altar made of scarlet and gold glass, only slightly lopsided. I looked over my shoulder at Shardas, who winked at me.

"One shouldn't break all the traditions at once," he rumbled.

I winked back, and gave my attention to Leontes.

He didn't talk about duty and responsibility, as a priest would have. He talked about love, and respect, and caring for each other always. Luka and I slipped rings onto each other's right hands: one on the third finger to symbolize fidelity, one on the fourth to symbolize love.

Then we kissed, and Leontes bowed, and Velika stepped forward. She spread her wings over us like a canopy, and blessed us as only the queen of the dragons could: that we would have long life, and prosperity, and children to bring us joy.

Then we kissed again, and everyone cheered, and the banquet began. As we danced later, under the two moons and the sparkling stars, I thought that I had never had a more perfect day.

"You see," Luka breathed in my ear, "that dress is not cursed."

"I just needed to find the right time to wear it," I said, laying my head on his shoulder.

"The right person to wear it with," he corrected me.

We became aware of a dragon staring at us.

"Hello!" Feniul grinned at us. Ruli was sleeping on top of his head, and Pippin yawned delicately from between his foreclaws. "Would you like to see your surprise now?"

Butterflies began a furious twirl in my stomach. "I suppose so." I felt a sudden dampness on Luka's palms.

"Feniul," Shardas said, overhearing, "I said *I* wanted to take them."

"But that I could come," Feniul reminded his cousin.

"Very well."

We said our good-byes to our family and friends; then we got on Shardas's back, and with Feniul following, flew to the eastern side of the island.

A little house gleamed in the moonlight, set perfectly on the shore of a peaceful lagoon. The walls were made of beautifully carved stone, and the roof was of shining multicolored glass.

"I wish you every happiness in the world, Creel," Shardas said as he set us down. "You deserve it."

"As do you," I said, hugging his neck as best I could.

"My life has never held more joy," he told me in his deep, rocky voice.

"Nor has mine," I agreed, and let Luka lead me into our little cottage on the shore of the dragons' home.

The New Palace at Dawn

"Y ou look radiant," Isla told me as I slid down off my horse in the courtyard of the New Palace.

"So do you," I said slyly.

She blushed and put one hand over her stomach in an unconscious gesture. Miles came forward to give me a hug, blushing as well.

"Now remember," Miles whispered as Luka dismounted and joined us. "We kept our promise: no one knows about the wedding in the Far Isles. So I hope you're ready to do it all over again, only this time with a thousand *human* guests and a regular priest!"

"We told everyone that we had gone to my home in Dranvel to see the sheep festival," Isla said.

"Oh, yes, it will all be wonderful!" I said, with an airy wave of my hand.

It hardly mattered now. Luka and I were married, and the people and dragons most important to us had been there. We had spent the last six weeks lounging in the Far Isles, playing with Velika and Shardas's hatchlings, as well as Amacarin and Gala's, who had hatched while we were rescuing Velika. I had had Marta and Alle send me back some white satin when they returned to the King's Seat, and had nearly finished stitching yet another wedding gown. This one was very simple, but rather elegant, and Luka was teasing me that I would put myself out of business by starting a fashion for embroidery-less gowns.

Now I could stand easily in my pure, white dress and smile while King Caxel glared away.

"But what's taking up most of Father's time is the trade negotiations," Miles said with a mysterious smile.

"What trade negotiations?" Luka glanced at the main doors of the palace, where news of our arrival was bringing a slew of servants and would no doubt soon rouse the king himself, despite the early hour.

"It seems that Moralienin traders are bringing some very interesting things to market," Miles said.

"Like exotic pet birds," Isla said with a giggle.

"Strange fruits, and scented woods," Miles added. "It's sparked some heavy trading among the Citatians as well, and the Roulaini. Merchants are sailing night and day, and Father wants a piece of the profits."

"Does he realize where these things are coming from?"

I felt a flutter of anxiety in my stomach. I had seen some of the dragons heading out toward the Moralienin trade routes with baskets on their backs, but hadn't wanted to interfere. I still thought it was too soon for the dragons to reveal the varieties available in the Far Isles.

"It's the worst-kept secret in the world," Isla said, rolling her eyes. "The Moralienin are calling the birds 'dragon-birds,' and half the fruits are named something like 'dragon-melons' or 'dragoneye berries.' But His Majesty has apparently decided to ignore that, and is making arrangements with Tobin to have the first pick of his clan's shipments."

I let out a small moan. "But the Far Isles . . . people will come looking . . ." I grabbed Luka's hand for support, and he squeezed back.

"Creel," Miles said in his kind way, "no one is going to want to trespass on the lands of thousands of dragons. The rumor is that only the Moralienin are powerful enough—or foolish enough—to trade with dragons, that every one of their ships is met by a battalion of a hundred dragons, armed with black spears twice the length of a man." Miles waggled his eyebrows. "Tobin and I started that last rumor ourselves."

I dropped Luka's hand so I could hug my brother-in-law again. He patted my back.

"They'll be safe, Creel," Luka said. "Don't worry."

"I know, I can't help it." I sighed.

"There are other things to worry about," Isla said, with a breathless little laugh. She was looking up at the doors to the palace.

Framed in the grand entryway was King Caxel, and just to his left was Aunt Reena. They came down the stairs together, and both of them started to talk before they even reached the bottom.

"So you remembered your duties at last," King Caxel huffed at Luka.

"Again I find you flaunting your legs in public," Aunt Reena shrieked, and threw a dressing gown around me. She'd apparently brought it with her, just for this purpose.

"Much to be done," King Caxel went on. "The new trade liaisons from Citatie and Moralien will be attending the wedding, and the feasts will begin next week."

"There are ungrateful girls wherever I look," Aunt Reena said. "I find good, noble husbands for Pella and Leesel, and how do they thank me? Elopements!"

I had been prepared to ignore my aunt's ranting, but this caught my attention.

"Pella and Leesel *eloped*? With whom?"

"Their horrid, little, common suitors from Carlieff came in the night and carried them both off last week!" Aunt Reena threw up her hands in despair. "Now you'll have two fewer bridal attendants, and I'll have to start finding matches for the younger girls," she grumbled.

My uncle joined us, hugging Luka and me, and kissing the top of my head. "Reena, dear, I still think that after Creel's wedding we should return to Carlieff and make sure our older girls are settled with their new husbands. We can always return to the King's Seat next year for a brief visit." He winked at me, and I grinned.

"We'll see," Aunt Reena said reluctantly. "I'm half-tempted to cut those girls off without a penny of my fortune."

I couldn't help but snort at this. What fortune? I certainly hoped that Aunt Reena wasn't hoping to negotiate a bride price for me from King Caxel.

"Don't you make that face at me, my girl!" She shook a finger under my nose. "I'm a wealthy trader now!"

"It's true," my uncle said in bemusement. "Both the monkeys and the dragon-birds are selling very well."

"The monkeys and the dragon-birds?" I drew back, exchanging looks with Luka.

"Horrid things," King Caxel said, shuddering. "But they do bring in gold, don't they, Reena?"

He and my aunt nodded like old business partners.

"Your aunt convinced one of these Moralienin traders to give her a dragon-bird and a monkey as gifts for the family of the new princess," my uncle explained. "And within a week, the monkey had given birth to two babies, and the dragon-bird had laid four eggs. Reena's been very savvy about it, selling a few, keeping the others to breed. Our rooms are quite full of small animals at this point." He pulled back a sleeve and showed us some bright red scratches that were clearly the work of Ruli's kin.

"Oh," I said, unable to think of anything else to say. I fervently hoped that they would take their burgeoning menagerie with them when they returned to Carlieff. I was not keen on either monkeys or the so-called dragon-birds.

"And where is your brother?"

My aunt had just noticed that Hagen hadn't returned with us. He was staying in the Far Isles to continue his apprenticeship, since he'd already seen me married once.

"Let's go inside and rest," Luka said, taking my arm and leading me toward the stairs.

"Creelisel, I asked you a question!"

"Hagen's going to be an alchemist," I said over one shoulder."

"An alchemist! An *alchemist*?!"

"I think we should live above the shop after the wedding,"

Luka whispered. "Although, Mordrel has offered to sell me their manor here in the King's Seat. They hardly use it anymore."

"Lovely," I said.

"Luka, I am expecting you to take part in finalizing the trade negotiations this afternoon," King Caxel called out.

"That will give me time to finish my latest wedding gown," I said.

"You'll be our liaison to the Moralienin," his father went on.

"Oh, good," Luka said to me. "You like to travel, and Tobin and Marta can come with us."

"I wonder how long it will be before we're trading directly with Shardas," I said.

"If it chances to take us months to return from Moralien, we can always claim that our ships are being blown off course," Luka pointed out.

"An excellent plan," I agreed, leaning my head on his shoulder as we left behind the sound of my aunt and his father, and passed into the great hall of the New Palace. "I wonder how soon you'll be needed in Moralien," I mused. "I would like to have our firstborn in the Far Isles. . . ."

ACKNOWLEDGMENTS

It is just and fitting that this book be dedicated to Amy Finnegan, because without her, Creel and Shardas might never have been launched on the world. She introduced me to my editor, and has been there ever since to read manuscripts with her keen critical eye and generally cheer me on. One fine day Amy and I met at Carl's Jr. to discuss her thoughts on *Dragon Flight*, which she had just read in manuscript form. And it was there, sitting at a sticky table in the play area while I tried to shove bites of star-shaped chicken nuggets into my toddler, that she gave me the idea for *Dragon Spear*.

Yep. The play area of Carl's Jr.

The french fry–redolent air was heady with inspiration, and by the time we left, I had a rough plot outline in my head.

Thank you, Amy! This one's for you!

But a book takes more than an author, a good friend, and some fast food to write. It also takes people like my fabulous editor, Melanie, who has listened to me rave (and rant) about this book over the phone more than with any other book. Then there's my copy editor, Chandra Wohleber, who has the unenviable job of making sure that I don't play fast and loose with continuity or timelines and keeps track of every scale of every dragon (which I am prone to forget). She's been with me since *Dragon Slippers*, and isn't she wonderful?

A good book also takes a good agent, in my opinion, and I've got a great one. Thanks to my other Amy—Amy Jameson—who also has a keen critical eye (it's a gift with these Amys!) and keeps me focused on the project at hand. (And somehow she does this all with two cute little ones underfoot!)

And speaking of cute little ones, I now have two myself! Thanks to the Boy, who continued to nap in the afternoons until the ripe age of three and a half, which allowed me to get a lot of work done even though I was deathly ill while writing most of this book. Baby Girl, who was the reason I was deathly ill, has made up for it by being cute and sleeping like a log. My husband and the rest of my family were wonderful as always: putting up with the mood swings caused by writing a book (and being pregnant) and watching Boy for me so that I could do some marathon writing. . . .

I'd never have made it without you!

Now let's all head out to Carl's Jr. and have some fries and a shake!

Jessica Day George is the author of many books for young readers, including the Dragon Slippers series; *Sun and Moon, Ice and Snow*; *Princess of the Midnight Ball*; and *Princess of Glass*. Jessica studied at Brigham Young University and worked as a librarian and bookseller before turning to writing full time. She now lives with her family in Salt Lake City, Utah.

www.JessicaDayGeorge.com